Caleb and Me

Doug Nelson (signature)

Doug Nelson

Detselig Enterprises Ltd.
Calgary, Alberta, Canada

Caleb and Me

© Doug Nelson, 1995

Canadian Cataloguing in Publication Data

Nelson, Doug (Douglas A.), 1950–
  Caleb and me

  ISBN 1-55059-126-6

  1. Cowboys--Fiction. I. Title.
PS8577.E44C3 1995   C813'.54   C95-910513-1
PR9199.3.N44C3 1995

Detselig Enterprises Ltd.
210, 1220 Kensington Road N.W.
Calgary, Alberta T2N 3P5

Cover Illustration by Don Inman
Cover Design by Dean MacDonald

The following stories within this volume have been previously published or broadcast: "Brahma," broadcast May, 1990 on Access Radio's *From the Banff Centre*; rebroadcast Nov. 17, 1991 on CBC Radio's *Alberta Anthology*; printed Jan. 1995 in *Simmental Trails*. "Scaregoose," broadcast Dec. 19, 1993 on CBC Radio's *Alberta Anthology*; "Mothers," printed in Regina-based literary magazine *green's magazine*; "Winter of '49," broadcast Jan. 21, 1990 on CBC Radio's *Alberta Anthology*, printed Jan. 1992 in *Grainews* and in Fall 1992 in Coteau Books' (Regina) *200% Cracked Wheat*.

Printed in Canada   SAN 115-0324   ISBN 1-55059-126-6

For my Mother,
Mildred Nelson

Contents

Acknowledgements

The author gratefully acknowledges the support of the Banff Centre for the Arts; with special thanks to my gentle editor, Rachel Wyatt, and Don Coles. I am also grateful to the Alberta Foundation for the (Literary) Arts for their financial support.

I extend a further thank you to family and friends who so kindly read and critiqued my stories, and encouraged me to write more.

Detselig Enterprises Ltd. appreciates the financial assistance for its 1995 publishing program provided by the Department of Canadian Heritage, Canada Council and the Alberta Foundation of the Arts, a beneficiary of the Lottery Fund of the Government of Alberta.

COMMITTED TO THE DEVELOPMENT OF CULTURE AND THE ARTS

*W*in ter of '49

The first two weeks of November my hound Caleb and me tramped out every morning looking for game. But we didn't see anything bigger, not even a track, than a rabbit or a squirrel. Every day the air was colder than the day before, and every day the country got quieter, and every day Caleb and me came home earlier.

Finally, near the middle of the month Old Man Winter quit fooling around and really threw us into the deep freeze. This one morning Caleb and me only made it a couple hundred steps from the door before that hoary-bearded old eunuch reached right through my red woolies and latched onto my ankles. As those icicle fingers crawled up my pants I turned around and legged it back for the shack.

It's lucky Caleb hustled his tail and scratched on the door. By the time Ma opened up we were so stiff she had to jerk us both across the threshold.

The next morning Caleb and me and the wife and all three boys woke up under one blanket. After she stoked the fire Ma figured she'd best get me and Caleb out of bed. She was talking about sending us out hunting again, but heck, I was still numb from the day before and it sure hadn't chinooked over night. Caleb and me fought to stay under the covers, but the kids kicked us out. As we thumped down on either side of the bed, the dog and me made a run for the stove, but Caleb was closer and he skittered under it first.

There wasn't much use hiding. Though we whined considerably, right after breakfast the old lady pushed my dog and me out the door.

It was quiet as a Saint's conscience out there, and the air was so cold that it felt like we were inhaling little slivers of sharp ice. I looked down at Caleb and he looked up at me. I shook my head and we started down the trail.

I was walking about as fast as a kid to his bath and hadn't made more than thirty steps when I turned to look for Caleb. And wasn't he a sight! That dog had stiffened up into about the nicest point position I ever did see. His nose was pointed ahead, with one paw tucked up under his chin, and his tail was sticking out the back pointing straight towards the cabin door. I just stood there staring and froze up stiff as a tree trunk myself.

I guess the wife, she noticed that we weren't back after a few minutes and sent a kid out with a rope so they could pull us in. Ma said I was solid and white, like one of those Greek marble statues. I kind of clunked up against the door stop and they had to lift me up and carry me over to the stove. They were none too careful though – not having much experience yet in handling frozen folks – and when they bumped my head against the threshold they chipped a piece off the top of my left ear.

Poor old Caleb, he wasn't so lucky. The kids brought him in after me so they were careful at the door, but when they stuffed him under the stove, one of them gave an extra shove. Snapped his tail right off! Didn't leave the poor hound with so much as a stump to wag with.

Now I can't speak for Caleb but after going through that thawing out process, I almost wished they had left me froze. It was just lucky that the stove was small and they could only thaw a bit of me at a time. Since they started with my feet, my frozen numbed head wasn't getting the tingling, thawing-out messages from my toes: I didn't feel anything until up around my armpits. But when I did! Well, it sure makes me sympathize with those folks that they're freezing and preserving nowadays. If they ever get thawed they're all going to feel that tickling, tingling in their heads like I did that day.

The wife, she said that it was lucky I had a brain no bigger than a peanut shell, otherwise I might not have been able to stand her – the thawing pain that is.

After that last trip, even Ma figured we should wait until it warmed up before Caleb and me went hunting again. I doubt she could have got Caleb to go anyway. Even after he was thawed out he never moved for the longest time, just lay hunkered under the stove with his broke off tail tucked between his front paws.

Me, I started spending a lot of time sitting in front of the stove, turning around and around in my chair like a rabbit on a spit. As a matter of fact we all five of us got to doing that: just sitting and turning like a bunch of loony folk. By spring those chair legs were wore down to stubs and the soles of our boots were thin as butter paper.

Turning round and round got to be pretty wearisome so once in a while I'd spit a shot of Old Mule chewing tobacco up on top of the stove. Then we'd watch those drops sizzle and hop around like a bunch of brown little kids with hot feet. The wife she didn't appreciate my dirtying her stove top, but it got so as I could tell when the fire needed to be stoked by how high the tobacco juice jumped.

If the tobacco juice appeared to be losing steam one of the kids or the wife would dress up nice and warm and head over to get some more fuel from the wood box. Even though the box was inside the door, the wood got so cold that a kid could crack a couple blocks together and they'd split into chunks just the right size for the stove. You couldn't hit those blocks too hard though, or the wood broke into a thousand splinters, and we sure didn't need kindling that winter of '49. The fire Ma started in the fall was an eternal flame that burned day and night until crocus time.

As snow-melt water was pretty dear, Ma got the once a day dishwashing habit out of her head real quick. We just chipped our plates off after each meal until, after about a week, the plates got too disgusting – even for Caleb and me. About that time we usually needed more fuel from the woodshed anyway.

On wash-and-wood day everybody kept busy. The wife, she scrubbed the dishes in a pan on the stove and set them in the warming cabinet to dry. At the same time the kids were fetching blocks of fuel from the woodshed outside. One of the boys would run out and grab an armful of blocks and start back. When he froze up, the other two pulled him in with a rope tied around his waist, hopefully with his stiffened up arms still glommed onto the wood. Then they waited till that first one thawed a bit and another one took a turn and ran out to get another armload. The thawing out part slowed things down so it took those boys most of an afternoon to fill the woodbox.

When the wife had finished washing the dishes it was time to dump the dishwater. Now you might not figure that dumping the dishwater was worth mentioning, but it took some doing that winter of '49.

We'd have to get the pan of water bubble-boiling before the wife grabbed it with her hot mitts. Then I'd take a run for the door and throw it open just before Ma went barrelling out at full gallop – we only made a bit of a timing mistake once all winter and I sure was glad Ma's arms stiffened up as quick as they did. Anyway, like I was saying, the wife, she'd go through the door like a stampeding buffalo and about the time I'd look around the corner she'd be heaving the water out of the dishpan in slowww motion.

.As soon as the pan was emptied I'd start pulling on the rope to haul her back into the shack. First, though, I'd have to give a jerk to detach her and the lip of the pan from the big arch of frozen dishwater. One especially cold day I had to get the kids to help me tug her loose as she'd been kind of slow and had only half-emptied the pan before everything stiffened up. It took a lot of jerking to get her loose. For a while there we thought maybe one of her skinny arms would give before the ice, but finally the ice broke.

After that extra long trip Ma got a taste of what I felt when I had my whole body unfroze. Because of her peanut brain remark

I was tempted to thaw her out head first, but then I remembered which end her mouth was on, so we took her nice and easy and slow, feet to head. That's probably the quietest two hours I ever spent with Ma. When she thawed out, the wife decided the dishes could stay dirty a week longer and the boys could start earlier and haul more wood in so we only needed a wash-and-wood day every second week.

I've got to admit I missed seeing those big arches of icy dishwater once a week. With the winter's sun shining behind them, those boiling bubbles would just sparkle; and when the sun sank low the arches got colored up like a winter's rainbow. It made washing day something to look forward to. The wife – she never did have time for ass-thetics – she still didn't like washing day. She said she never saw anything anyway because her eyeballs got all frizzed up with the steam and the frost.

Ma's eyes weren't the only things that got steamed and frosted on washing day. There were two windows on either end of the old shack but by the first of December there was an inch of frosting stuck to each one of them. We only got a look outside on wood and wash days. Heck, the whole darned world could have blown up out there and we wouldn't have known until the wood box was empty!

During that winter of '49 New Years passed by before we even noticed that we'd missed Christmas, but the kids didn't fret much seeing as we didn't have a turkey, and seeing as nobody would have wanted to go out and cut a tree anyway. I promised those boys that next year we'd have two trees, and two turkeys. The thought of turkeys made the boys' eyes spark. Since Caleb and me couldn't get out to bag a rabbit or squirrel, everybody got to dreaming of eating something besides deer meat.

By the end of January, though, venison was starting to look pretty good, because even it was getting scarce. By the middle of February we were gnawing twice-boiled soup bones.

Caleb still had his detached tail tucked between his paws, but he got to eying it, and sniffing it, and one day in February he was just about to chomp down on his own wagger when Ma cussed and jerked it away from him. That next pot of soup tasted pretty darned good. Caleb, he liked the leavings well enough himself, picking away with his teeth at a finger-thin line of tail bones.

That next day the kids were mumbling about roasts and steaks as they were turning around in front of the stove. I couldn't hear too well because of the scraping of the chair legs, but there was always at least one pair of those blue eyes sighting like a lighthouse lamp on my dog. Caleb was too busy chewing on the remains of his tail bone to notice, but I could tell that those boys of mine were figuring out where the T-bone was situated on a dog.

I craved a good feed myself, but the thought of roast Caleb with onions on the side didn't whet my appetite none. I explained to those boys that Caleb was a valuable hound. He could chase cows, he could hunt, he was a good-for-anything kind of dog. Him and me, we were a perfect pair that couldn't be broke up. I told those boys that I'd just as soon slice a chunk off my own haunch as put a knife to my canine partner. The kids seemed amenable to the change and proceeded to study my rear end.

I could see that our meat situation was getting pretty desperate – desperate enough to risk another trip outside. One of the boys had been hallucinating earlier that week. He had said that he saw rabbits out in the yard when he was gathering wood. He said that there were white ones all over outside. I'd laughed with the rest at the time, but now I played the story up. I said that we couldn't see out the frosted windows, and maybe there were rabbits all over outside, and that we wouldn't know for sure unless we looked.

The wife commented that maybe my peanut brain wasn't over the freezing yet and two of the kids laughed; but the character that had been hallucinating, he said he'd hold the rope if I wanted to go out and shoot one of those white rabbits he'd seen. Well I didn't have much choice, I dusted off my squirrel gun and pulled on every coat and sweater I had. As I headed towards the door, Caleb backed farther under the stove, and I went out alone.

It was squinty-eyed bright afternoon, but the sun didn't have a matchstick's worth of heat to it. The country looked like it was made of crystal glass and if a fellow hollered too loud every glittery thing would shatter and tinkle down onto the snow. I stood staring so long I almost forgot to look for imaginary rabbits. But just before my eyes frosted over, I saw them. They were hard to pick out white on white, but looking close I could see pairs of button-black eyes and pink-edged ears. The rabbits were huddled together in the snow all around the outside of the shack. Like a darned fool I let my mouth drop open and froze up stiff as a popsicle before I could get a shot off.

Since my eyes were bugged out and my mouth was wide open when they pulled me in, Ma and the boys figured I must have seen something. While I was thawing out Ma wiped the gun with kerosene so it'd fire in the cold. Then she shoved me out the door again.

I kept my mouth shut this time and edged up to one of those big-eared varmints. He didn't look like he'd be moving too fast but I wanted to be close enough so's I could just fall on him after I fired. That white rabbit was sitting full centred in my sights when I pulled the trigger.

"Kee-rack!" There was a puff of smoke, but instead of firing the whole darned gun blew apart. The lead bullet stayed in one piece; it dropped and rolled down between the rabbit's paws. He was sniffing it when I toppled over and wrapped my arms around him. A live rabbit don't carry like a block of wood, though. The beggar squeezed out of my stiff arms before Ma could pull me inside.

The wife and kids weren't too pleased with pulling me in empty handed again; but, because I had a bit of rabbit fur caught in my mitts, they were willing to give me another shot. As soon as I was close to thawed they started shoving me towards the door. I braced one foot against each side of the jamb and said I didn't have a gun. Ma handed me the 30.30, but I braced myself again and told her that my heart was starting to act up with all this freezing and unfreezing. I said that this would probably be my last trip, and didn't a man get one last wish before he went to meet his Maker – all I wanted was to sit in front of the stove for a minute or two with a fresh chew of tobacco.

The wife, she ain't all bad. She quit pushing, cut off a plug of Old Mule and let me sit down to enjoy a turn or two in front of the stove. But I only got in one spit before Ma jerked me off the chair and hustled me out the door again.

Now I knew there wasn't any use trying to shoot. Even if the gun did fire, a 30 calibre bullet would blow a hopper to smithereens. The only thing I could think of doing was to use the gun as a club. I had to act fast before I stiffened up so I lined up on a spot between the first two pink-edged ears I saw. That old rifle whistled through the cold air and landed smack dab between those ears.

Unfortunately, they weren't a matched pair. My Winchester shattered from stock to muzzle between two rabbits sitting side by side.

That was the last straw. First my dog lost his tail, and now both my guns were gone. In utter disgust I spat out my whole chew of tobacco. That pear-shaped plug arched through the air towards one of them rabbits and plunked down right between his ears. The old hopper he hunkered up like he was about to jump, and then keeled over – fresh killed and fresh froze all in one shot. I can't say I wasn't a little sorry to get the poor beggar that way, but it surely was either him, or me, or Caleb on the supper table that night. Anyway, I toppled onto that rabbit and tucked him into me like those football players do nowadays.

It didn't take me long to thaw out but when I did there was nothing but bones left, and the boys and Caleb were gnawing on them. The wife, she was smiling. She said that was the best rabbit she'd ever ate.

Well, I'd found a sure fire way of getting those rabbits and I don't suppose I wasted more than two or three plugs through the rest of the winter. It was darned lucky that I'd stocked up on Old Mule in the fall. When the first chinook finally blew in, I was down to my last pouch.

I still keep plenty of chewing tobacco around the place, and I always stock up special heavy in the fall. A fellow never knows when there might come another one like the winter of '49.

Mothers

My two little grandaughters stared up at me, wide eyed. "Gee Grandpa," Patti said, "That must have been really cold." She shivered, then she pouted her bottom lip and looked at me with sad eyes, "but, those poor bunnies . . . "

". . . And Caleb," added Katie. "Was it Daddy who pushed him so hard under the stove, and broke off his tail? . . . Poor Caleb."

Both girls kneeled down and started stroking my dog, but when they tried to touch his tail he tucked in the stub and sat up on his haunches.

Just as Caleb sat up, the screen door slammed and Emeline stepped down the house steps packing a tray that held a plate of still-steaming oatmeal cookies and three tall glasses of chocolate milk and a bowl of white for Caleb.

"Grandma! Grandma!" the girls yelled, as them and Caleb jumped up and run to meet her.

"Grandpa told us about that really cold winter," said Katie, "when you got all frozen, and Caleb broke his tail."

"And when Grandpa spitted on those poor bunnies," added Patti.

Well now, before I could duck my head, Emeline caught my eye and I knew darned well there was a lecture on the way. She set the tray down and started explaining all about exaggerating to the twins, and the difference between real life and tall tales. I knew darned well she was really aiming the message at me. It seems like older female creatures just don't take kindly to a fellow stretching the truth . . . even just a touch.

Once Emeline'd left us free to enjoy our snack, I decided I'd change my tune, I'd tell them girls some true-to-life stories, ones about things that really did happen to me and mine out in the Snake Valley country.

I started off by showing the girls a shot from our photo album, a picture of a couple of mothers from my early days. The picture showed my Mother holding my baby brother Ferris out in front of the big, hip-roofed barn at our old home place.

The other mother was peering around the corner of the barn. It was our red and white Ayrshire milk cow, Daisy.

When I was a youngster me and Daisy had a steady date beside the milking stool at six o'clock every morning and every night.

To begin with ours was one of those true mutually benefiting relationships. At each milking, Daisy got a gallon of chop, a forkful of green hay and the relief of my deflating her tight udder. Me, I had a warm spot in her flank to rest my forehead on, and dream against, and the opportunity to flex-strengthen my hands filling a foam-topped bucket of fresh milk. I can still hear those first thick white squirts spink-splonking into the pail's empty bottom.

Every morning and night Daisy'd be standing at the cow-pasture gate waiting to be let in. When I got close she'd moo to me soft and low, like I was her very own calf. And after I started milking, Daisy'd swing her head back to nuzzle my shoulder with a sweat-damp nose.

Caleb appreciated Daisy, too. Since she knew Caleb was my dog, Daisy didn't take a run at him like the other cows did, and she'd even let him belly up close behind her where I could aim long milky streams into his open mouth.

I got the first hint of our relationship going sour the summer's morning Daisy squirmed and switched her tail, and, instead of enjoying a warm drink, Caleb ended up spluttering and sneezing and pawing a milk moustache off his nose. I had been milking Daisy morning and night for almost a year, and that was the first time she'd ever got fussy. If the other cows were upset about something, they'd flick their long stringy tails in my face, sometimes kick over the pail or even splunk a foot into it. But Daisy had never made a wrong move – up until that day.

I was surprised and hurt so I told Pa. He came over to the barn, took a look at Daisy and informed Caleb and me that our big-bellied milk cow would soon be birthing a calf.

Well now, I was just about as pleased and excited as an eight year old, sort of first-time daddy could be. I told Pa that Caleb and me would head right on over to the barn and bed a stall for Daisy. I said we'd be happy to haul feed and water to her, and clean her stall twice a day if she could just stay in the barn until her time came.

But Pa said no. He said it was summertime, and since this wasn't Daisy's first calf, she'd be better off birthing outside in the cow-pasture. Caleb and me kept pestering, though, until Pa finally compromised. He said that Daisy usually wandered to the far end of the pasture the day before she calved, and when Caleb and me saw her down there by herself, he'd help us bring her in.

As soon as we got the okay from Pa, my dog and me hurried over to the barn. Our Belgian stud had the biggest and best boxstall in the barn, but he was still running out in the Buffalo Hills with the mares so Caleb and me commandeered his stall for Daisy.

I don't suppose there's ever been a milk cow that's had a nicer spot prepared for her birthing. On our trips back and forth from the straw pile, I had the wheelbarrow heaped so high that I couldn't even see over the yellow bedding. Caleb had to bark directions ahead of me as I weaved and wobbled a dozen wheelbarrow loads over to the barn. We fluffed the straw up so it was a nice level two foot deep, and finished off by portioning three gallons of chop into Daisy's feed bucket and forking her manger full of the freshest, greenest hay we could find.

In my mind I could see Daisy promenade into that stall, like the great British queen she was. A fellow wouldn't be able to see her legs or feet, not even her royal udder for the deep bedding. Her beauteous form would float over the clean yellow straw right across to the full manger, where Daisy could munch enough feed to fill up all four of her stomachs at once.

For the next couple days, before and after school I kept an eagle eye on the pasture – even though Pa had said he didn't think Daisy would "pop" for a while yet. They say a watched pot won't boil; well, the same thing goes for cattle – a watched cow won't pop either. By the weekend, Daisy was still hanging out with the other milk cows.

Saturday morning Caleb and me were supposed to be weeding and thinning the garden. Caleb was a bit careless as to what he dug and what he left, but he did work fast. Myself, I didn't get much done. I'd straighten up to check Daisy, then bend down to pull one more weed, straighten up again, then down . . . up and down, up and down, up and down. It's lucky I was young. If I tried bending like that now I'd probably kink and break into two pieces like a chunk of rusty fence wire.

About mid-afternoon, Daisy, by herself, ambled over against the far fence and lay down.

Well, as soon as her big belly touched ground I was up and running. Pa was rodweeding a summer-fallow field south of the house. In no time at all Caleb and me had dusted out into the field to tell him about Daisy.

Pa "whoa-ed" his outfit and gave the horses a breather while he heard me out. After I finished my spiel, Pa was surprisingly reluctant to help us retrieve Daisy. He said he figured the milk cow would wait until he brought his outfit in for supper. Just before clucking the horses on their way, Pa made me and Caleb promise to stay away from Daisy.

Well, there was nothing to do but shove my hands in my pockets and shuffle back to the garden, kicking dirt lumps on the way. Caleb, he ran ahead and made a quick, heavy cull of a half row of carrots before tuckering out. When I arrived my dog was lying with his muzzle resting on top of a potato hill, staring towards the cow pasture.

I started weeding again. All the time I worked, my mind dwelled on man's inhumanity towards milk cows – and about bull's inhumanity towards milk cows too. Pa had said that McCurdy's Highland bull was the calf's father. As I tore at each weed, then straightened, then tore again, I couldn't help but wonder where in the blazes that character was anyway. We hadn't seen hide nor hair of the gallivanting red devil for almost a year. He obviously wasn't fond of Daisy anymore, and he couldn't've been very concerned about his own flesh and blood either.

I figured that even if the beggar did straggle over for the birthing, I'd probably spit in his red face then sic Caleb on him. My dog and me could look after Daisy without help from that bull, without Pa even – if he'd just let us.

I was so steamed up that I scurried up and down those rows and finished the whole garden in less than an hour. When I was about to start a second cull, my apron-flapping Mother ran outside and dragged me away. She said she'd been watching me from the kitchen window, and she had a better use for my up-and-down routine.

She led me over to the pump in front of the house and I grabbed the pump handle. Once I got into a rhythm, my Mother said she'd never seen such a gush of water. It only took a matter of minutes for me to fill the house cistern. Then I ran over to the barn and filled the corral water trough to overflowing. My Mother could see I still had more pumping in me, so she led me back to the house and hooked up the garden's irrigating hose. In no time at all I'd pumped three or four inches of water onto the garden. Mother's face was just a-beaming as she moved her gushing hose over to where it would irrigate the grass around the house.

Every time I moved, Caleb would shuffle over close to where I was pumping, sigh and flop down – his nose pointed towards the cow pasture. I'd glance over, see Daisy lying out there, and pump harder than ever.

Not much before suppertime, Pa came long-striding into the yard behind his eight-horse hitch. Caleb and me were waiting for him. When Pa stopped the horses next to the fresh-filled water trough, I dodged in amongst dinner-plate-sized, hairy hooves unsnapping cross-checks. After Pa folded and hung the lines up, he stripped off bridles. When a horse was free, it would sip a drink of water, then lumber to the barn, duck into its stall and start munching supper.

Now I'd watched lots, but I'd never unharnessed a horse before. I figured that day was a good time to learn.

Old Brownie was as gentle as a big kitten, so I stepped into his stall. Both the hames' strap and the belly band were within a little fellow's reach. I unbuckled them both and started heaving and tugging, trying to pull that harness off Brownie's back.

When everything started to slide, Pa yelled, "Look out!" But he was too late. I dropped butt first onto the straw and the whole tangled mess tumbled on top of me.

Luckily the steel hames missed me, but I ended up sitting in the straw like a darn fool, with leather straps around my shoulders and the heavy tugs draped across my stomach and legs. Brownie stopped munching long enough to give me a disgusted glance, then turned back to his dinner.

After Pa rescued me, Caleb and me got relegated to watching, and to pacing up and down the alley.

When Pa finished, he saddled his riding horse. I swung onto my pony, and Caleb and me were about to head outside, when Pa said that we'd best leave the dog behind. I tried to talk him out of it but Pa insisted. He said a dog, even Caleb, would be upsetting to Daisy right then.

I lured my best friend inside a stall with that old favorite: "here boy, here's a bone" trick, then quickly latched both the top and bottom boxstall doors behind him. Caleb wasn't the least bit happy about being locked in. He whined and scratched at the door as me and Pa rode out to the cow pasture.

When we rode in close and made her get up, Daisy groaned her displeasure. On the way back to the barn she took slow, mincing steps, with her swollen gut wobbling like a water-balloon full to bursting, and everything floppy-loose under her lifted tail. Daisy didn't seem too keen on coming in. She angled this way and that, zigged and zagged across the pasture, but we finally manoeuvered her through the gate into the yard.

Caleb was still barking and whining and door scratching. He was making such a racket that we had trouble persuading Daisy to step into the barn. Pa finally told me to run inside and get that noisome hound out of the way.

I dragged Caleb by the scruff of his neck out the back door, while Pa herded Daisy in through the front. My dog and me didn't even get to see our dairy queen float into her stall.

Pa wouldn't let us visit Daisy after she was inside either. He said our milk cow was real close to calving and she'd been upset enough already by Caleb's serenading. He said we could see her in the morning when we did our chores.

Caleb, he whimpered and presented Pa with the saddest, sorriest pair of dog-eyes you ever did see and I argued till I was blue in the face, but Pa wouldn't give in – he wouldn't let us have even the teensiest look-in at Daisy.

You can bet Caleb and me didn't eat hardly anything for supper and didn't sleep much that night either. It felt like Christmas Eve, or the day before my birthday.

Caleb and me were both wide-eyed at four-thirty in the morning. By five o'clock I knew we weren't going to get any more shut-eye, so I pulled on my clothes and we sneaked down the stairs. I grabbed the milk pails, eased the screen door open, went out, then eased it shut, and Caleb and me hurried over to the barn.

Before I'd even slid the door open, the horses heard us and nickered. I shushed them quiet and promised that we would feed them – right after we looked in on Daisy. Caleb and me ran down the alley to the end of the barn.

The stud's stall was built with extra-thick planks and, to keep him from reaching out and biting other horses, there were iron prison bars sunk into its high-set windows.

The barred window next to the door was too high for me to peek over, so I set a three-legged milking stool where I could stand on it. Caleb tried to climb up on the stool before me but I shoved him off. Being human should count for something, and I figured getting the first look at Daisy was my privilege.

Even with the extra height of the stool, I couldn't much more than stick my nose over the lip of the sill. But by straining on tip-toes I could see Daisy's head and the top half of her back where she lay below the window.

When I spoke, Daisy stared up at me. Then she swung her head around and down to nuzzle something lying beside her. She mooed soft and low – like she used to moo at me.

I knew that Daisy must have calved, so I grabbed hold of the bars and lifted myself higher. And I could see it! The calf's sleeping head was curled into its flank. Its dark red hair was licked clean. That calf was a real beauty – except for the fact it favored McCurdy's Highland bull.

I ignored the unfortunate resemblance and cooed and talked baby talk, and told Daisy what a wonderful momma she was. But she just stared up at me like I was bonkers or something.

Meanwhile, Caleb was going nuts below me. That crazy dog whined and jumped and clawed the back of my legs. He even knocked the stool over, and I had to ease my way down, then drop the last couple inches to the alley floor.

I reset the stool and helped Caleb plant his hind legs on it. But, even hopping on tippy claws, my dog couldn't nudge his nose over the window sill. Caleb whined and complained until I lifted him up so he could look in. He pushed his nose through the bars and started simpering and whimpering at Daisy and her calf in the most disgusting fashion. I was embarrassed myself, and darned glad there were no other dogs around to hear whatever canine gibberish Caleb was spouting.

Back then my dog was almost as heavy as me. I couldn't hold him up for more that a minute or so. When I had to set him down Caleb gave me a sidelong pout, sniffed and slunk over to an open stall and lay down.

After pulling myself up by the bars for a second look, I decided I'd like to touch Daisy's calf. I dropped back down, unlatched the door and stepped inside.

Daisy's back end was towards me. I bent down and gave her a comforting scratch on the hip. Then, with my shoulder rubbing the rough plank wall, I edged along, talking slow and soft all the time until I was right across from Daisy's head. As I stroked behind her floppy ears, Daisy stiffened and scowled at me. She wouldn't bow her head to let me scratch the chaff out of the dust-collecting hollow behind her poll.

I lowered my hand to touch the sleeping calf and Daisy's cow eyes narrowed. She watched my every move.

As I touched the calf, I was newly amazed at how fine haired and silky-soft a newborn calf's skin felt. My fingers were just completing a second slow stroke when something creak . . . creaked.

It was the boxstall door. It creaked farther open, and this time Daisy noticed. She swung her head back and watched as Caleb squeezed his nose, his ears and his shoulders through the widening crack. Daisy's hind end rose like a puppeteer had jerked her strings, then her front legs pushed up. I was amazed as our meek, mild milk cow spun around, bawled and made a lowered-head rush for the door. Caleb stood staring at her too. He barely jumped out of the way when Daisy rammed the door wide open with her head.

But the most surprised of us all was Daisy's bug-eyed calf. The poor little beggar leapt up, echoed his momma's beller, and started butting me, bellering "Maaa . . . maaa," with every butt.

When Daisy swung her heavy head around and glared at me I knew I'd best get the heck out of there. And quick. But Daisy stood blocking the doorway. All I could think to do was to leap up and grab hold of the window bars – which I did, without the aid of the three-legged stool. My boots scrabbled up the wall and I crawled onto the window ledge.

Daisy stood below, watching to make sure I didn't set a foot in the boxstall – the very stall Caleb and me had specially prepared for her. Sitting scrunched on that narrow sill and looking out at the rest of the barn through the bars, I felt like Snake Valley's version of the Birdman of Alcatraz.

For a moment Caleb stood silhouetted in the open door at the other end of the barn. I cussed him. And then I told him that if he weren't one already, I'd trade him for a yellow dog and shoot the dog. That was my Pa's favorite saying and I figured it suited the occassion.

A couple minutes after I yelled at him I heard Caleb barking over at the house. Pretty soon Pa stepped through the barn door. He looked worried as he hurried down the alley. He was still shrugging his braces over his shoulders as he buttoned up his trousers.

After checking the stall, though, and finding both us youngsters safe, Pa couldn't help but chuckle. I can't say as I saw much humor in the situation – at least not until after Pa stepped inside and packed me on his shoulders past Daisy and out of the stall.

That fickle-hearted mother got to keep her calf for three or four days. Then Pa took it away for us kids to bottle feed, and I started milking Daisy again. For the first couple days she shifted from foot to foot and threatened to kick the pail, and kept swatting her tail in my face. But within a week Daisy'd stopped her fussing. By the end of August she was low-bellering to me at the gate and Caleb was sipping squirted milk again.

We were all bosom buddies until Daisy freshened again the next summer. When she did, Caleb and me still got excited, but we didn't bed a boxstall for her. That next year we let Daisy calve out in the cow-pasture by herself.

Trip to the Medicine Wheel

After I finished Daisy's story, I swiped a sleeve across my mouth, then watched as the girls wiped chocolate milk moustaches off their faces too.

One of the girls looked up at me. "Boy, Grandpa," she said with a smile, "I sure like listening to you."

"The pleasure's darned sure mine Miss Katie," I replied.

The little girl's smile turned to a pout-lipped frown, just like Emeline used to look when she was mad. "I'm not Katie," the twin blustered, "I'm Patti!"

The real Miss Katie looked just about as upset as her sister. She lectured me with her finger, "Grandma doesn't ever call us the wrong name."

"Nope," I said. "I don't suppose she does. Your Grandma's a pretty sharp cookie." I grinned down at the girls. "So how's about I tell you a story about me and your Grandma?"

The twins still looked a tad perturbed, but they nodded their heads.

"Well now, up until I quit in grade eight, me and my future wife – your Grandma – went all through school together. I recall a few passable days and a lot more uncomfortable ones, but me and your Grandma both agree on which was our most memorable school day."

Our teacher at that time, Miss Edith Quail, had come to Snake Valley a couple years earlier, when she was seventeen years old and fresh-squeezed from Normal School. Right from the start Miss Quail was no shrinking violet. She spent the first morning of her first year lecturing us kids about how important schooling was for getting ahead in the world. She ended her talk by saying how she considered educating us rural kids a sacred trust bestowed upon her by the Snake Valley School Board.

Miss Quail was a husky, hot-blooded young lady who could wield an awful mean strap when the need arose. If our offences were relatively minor, Miss Quail would rap our knuckles, or our knuckleheads with a hardwood pointer. And if a trouble-maker required immediate attention, and the missile was handy, Miss Quail proved to be a fair-to-middling shot with a chalk brush. Although she might not have commanded our undivided attention at all times, Miss Quail always had us kids' fearful respect.

But the reason me and Emeline remember Miss Quail wasn't because she was any nastier – or nicer – than the other teachers; not even because she lasted longer than most – three years. No, the main reason we remember Miss Edith Quail was because of that one aforementioned school day.

In early March of Miss Quail's third (and last) year, our school suffered a general infestation of head lice. All of us boys and most of the girls had to be shaved bald before being treated. For the next couple months, under their kerchiefs and bonnets, the girls were bristle-haired and brush cut just like us boys. The only two exceptions were Dessie Nordmark, whose Mother rinsed her long, blond hair regularly with coal oil, and Patsy Miller, who was most likely just as infested as the rest of us, but wasn't shaved because she was Miss Quail's pet student.

Spring is a time of the year when school kids just naturally tend to perk up; and if you add the fact that most of our heads itched from a new growth of hair, it's quite likely that by April we were more rambunctious that normal. I know she'd had to limit our trips up to the pencil sharpener to noon hour, otherwise there was always a kid standing up by the window, staring outside and turning the crank handle, with Miss Quail's mouth twitching at each grind . . . grind . . . grind. But Miss Quail's discipline problems took a definite turn for the worst one particular Friday.

Because the morning was frosty cold, Miss Quail had built a snap-crackling, hot fire in the school's potbellied stove. By the time she jangled her bell for morning classes, though, a warm chinook wind was blowing from the west. By eleven o'clock, with help from the sun's rays slanting through our three east windows, the big boxy schoolroom had got awful warm . . . and a tad smelly.

Most of us boys came from farms, and spattered on our pant legs was Snake Valley gumbo mixed with the malodorous remains of a week's choring. After an hour or so, even our hardy nostrils twitched to the smell of soured milk and horse, cow, chicken and pig manure. Those simmering odors overpowered the regular schoolroom aroma of chalk dust and ink and fresh paper, and was working on the tang of the spring-soft apples in our lunch tins and the whiff of coal oil scent from Dessie Nordmark's long blond hair.

A big, fat housefly appreciated the warmth and aroma. After wriggling out of its winter's crack, the bloated bluebottle first tapped away at the east-facing window panes for a minute, then lazily buzzed from the row of little kids' desks at the front, down and around the aisles to big kids' desks at the back.

The fly set down on my brother Philmore's muck-stiff pantleg. It rubbed its skinny front legs together then flicked a curly-Q tongue out at a tasty morsel. Philmore took a swat at the fly. He missed, but speeded its progress back up the aisle toward the front of the class. Miss Quail turned and swiped at the slow-buzzing nuisance, but she missed too, and we all watched as the big bluebottle lazily spiralled up and up, past the blackboard, up over the map rolls, all the way up to the portrait of King George, where it settled with a fly-sigh on the oak frame just under the royal gentleman's beard.

Philmore leaned across the aisle and whispered something to Patsy Miller. Whatever Philmore said got both Patsy and Dessie

Nordmark giggling. Although the chalk brush was handy, Miss Quail just glared them quiet – Patsy was her pet remember – then carried on with a long division lesson for us grade fives: me and Dessie and Emeline Palandine.

The blackboard filled the front wall, and wrapped around both corners, so it covered the front half of the schoolroom. That morning Miss Quail had scribbled over almost all her board space in an attempt to keep us kids interested. She'd even used some of her precious pink and yellow chalk for circling important facts and figures.

Outside, the chinook wind whined around the corners of the school.

The room was getting hotter and gamier, and us kids were getting restless. Even model students like Emeline were squirming to keep their bottoms from sticking to the wood benches. The stifling hot atmosphere wasn't real conducive to learning.

The conditions weren't much better for teaching. Miss Quail's shoes clacked and squeaked on the varnished floor as she walked back and forth to chalk numbers on the blackboard. Sweat marks formed on her yellow blouse, one running down the middle of her back, and another one down from under her writing arm.

Finally Miss Quail let out a disgusted sigh. She dropped her arm, turned to us and said: "Noon recess will be a half hour early today children. You may leave the room."

Don't think we weren't ready to go. Books slapped shut and desk legs scraped as everybody got up and crowded out the door. We ran down the steps and into the schoolyard, squealing like wiener pigs let free of a dirty stall. Once we were outside we sucked in, then laughed out, long breaths of the clean chinook air.

But my brother Philmore and his best friend, Cross Harmon, weren't enjoying the fresh air. Miss Quail had latched onto them to help her air the room out. We heard her and the boys grunting as they heaved on the stubborn windows. The School Board had financed a painting bee in the fall, and white paint must've got brushed on too thick around the window sills. Miss Quail and her crew couldn't pry even one open.

Our frustrated teacher had to give up on her airing out idea, but not without spewing words that we kids were surprised she even knew, or let alone used. Things like: "For Pete's sake!"; "Good Lord Jesus why?!" and even "Damn!"

Philmore and Cross must have been surprised at her language too because they scuttled out the door with hands over their mouths to keep from laughing.

Miss Quail stalked out after the boys. She bent down and propped the door open with a grade six reader, then called Cross back over to her. After grilling him for half a minute, she brushed the blowing hair wisps from her face, and announced that Cross would lead us on an afternoon field trip to see the Indians' Medicine Wheel. She told us to eat our lunches right away so we could get an early start.

Miss Quail tramped down the stairs and marched back to her little storeroom-office behind the school. The door slammed shut behind her. Now that I think back, it could've been the wind slammed the door shut. Actually, it could've been the wind caused a lot of difficulties that day. I've heard it said that Europeans do some crazy things when that foehn wind is blowing full blast out of the Alps. I know my dog Caleb, he can get a kind of glazed look in his eye when a chinook's blowing.

Anyway, us kids had to run back inside the school to get our lunch buckets from the cloakroom. Because it was close, I grabbed Emeline's syrup pail and handed it to her so she could get back out into the fresh air. Sometimes it doesn't take much to please a woman. Emeline gave me just about the sweetest smile I ever saw for that one little favor. Now, starlings are not one of my personal favorite birds, but I understand the males of that species have an interesting habit of decorating their nest with flowers to attract a female. I consider that act of handing over the lunch bucket as one of the first flowers that attracted Emeline to my nest.

Of course, me and Emeline didn't sit together for lunch or anything like that. The girls always ate down at the swing and teeter-totter end of the schoolyard and us boys bunched up over against the horse pasture fence. But that particular noon-break, Emeline walked from the girls side, across the ball diamond and straight towards us boys.

I can still see her coming: a little wisp of a thing, smiling, with her kerchiefed-head held high, holding her free hand behind her to keep her powder-blue dress from blousing up in the breeze, and the other hand holding two of her mother's melt-in-your-mouth, shortbread cookies. She stepped right up to me and offered me the cookies; said she couldn't finish all her lunch.

Boy did I get kidded about having a sweetie, but those cookies were worth it. I ate the first one before Emeline made it back to the girls' side, but the second one I just took small bites and nibbled at.

By the time I finished the second cookie, the rest of the boys had tapped the tops back on their empty lunch tins. Since Miss Quail still hadn't made an appearance and since we were going to be gone for a while and wouldn't be riding, Philmore and Cross Harmon and a couple other older boys decided to take their ponies down for a drink at the spring. I trailed along behind, leading our buggy mare, Belle.

We were almost to the bottom of the hill, when I looked back up and saw Dessie Nordmark and Patsy Miller following us, their long dresses and hair flapped in the wind.

Our school was built on top of a knoll and the spring-fed water trough was located at the bottom, in behind a patch of diamond willows. Philmore and Cross and the other boys led their mounts around the bushes and over to the wooden trough. The horses dipped their noses in the spring-clear water and started slurping. Me and Belle were still waiting our turn when the two girls, hand in hand, skipped around the bushes. Dessie Nordmark was Snake Valley's prettiest girl (next to Emeline, of course), but "four-eyes" Patsy Miller wasn't even in the running. That day though, Patsy was sporting the kind of smile that makes a fellow's knees buckley. She looked like she figured she was pretty, and by thinking that way, Patsy's face glowed every bit as strong as Dessie's.

The two girls separated, clasped their hands behind their backs and sauntered towards the trough. The chinook tugged and flicked their long hair, and pushed their skirts tight against their legs.

Philmore and Cross jerked their horses' heads out of the water, stepped back and slapped the reins into my hand. The other three fellows did the same, and I was left holding a half dozen horses.

That pack of boys was all wolf eyes. The two girls flashed them a pair of cheek-dimpling smiles, then giggled and sidled toward the willows. As the boys eased after them, Patsy stumbled and fell. Cross and Philmore pounced, each one grabbed an arm to help lift Patsy up. The other three fellows circled Dessie – just in case she lost her balance too.

With the two boys holding her arms, Patsy had trouble resetting her tilted glasses so Philmore and Cross let go. They dropped their hands to their sides.

A couple of the horses, their tails swooshing in the wind, had shifted in front of me. I had to kneel and peer between Belle's legs to watch what happened next.

Patsy looked from Philmore to Cross and back again, radiating the full force of her knee-buckling smile. My brother never lacked gumption. While Patsy gazed over at Cross, Philmore leaned forward and kissed her on the cheek. Patsy's face flushed a full colored, sliced-beet red. She clasped her hands together, squirmed and let out a loud, squeaky giggle.

One of Dessie's three admirers got brave too. Billy Strum pecked her on the cheek. Dessie giggled, but not as squeaky or as loud as Patsy. Right away Dessie's other beaus, the buck-toothed Horvath twins, they decided to get in on the act. Standing on either side of her, the twins puckered and pecked – like a pair of hens after the same kernel of wheat. Dessie tried focusing a blue eye on either twin, but she couldn't manage it, so she ducked and the brothers' buckteeth clacked together. They grabbed at their mouths and started to cuss one another.

I was hunched up under Belle just a-smiling. I figured I might get to go in as a substitute for one, or both, of the Horvaths.

It was definitely Cross and Patsy's turn next, though. It turned out Cross Harmon wasn't a cheek pecker. When he leaned over, Cross set his lips smack dab onto Patsy's. And he left them there for a while. Behind her thick-lensed glasses, Patsy's eyes had time to close. When Cross finally eased away, the girl's puckered, pouting lips followed his. The rest of her leaned that way too. If Philmore hadn't grabbed her from behind, Patsy would have toppled right into Cross's arms.

Lord knows what all this might have led to if Miss Quail hadn't marched around the willows right then. She slapped her hands on her hips and shouted, "My good God! What are you doing?! Stop it this minute!" Cross, he grinned at our teacher and took a step back. Philmore's mouth and his hands opened. He let an overbalanced Patsy drop free. She landed nose first in the grass at Cross's feet. Dessie, still down on her knees, reached up and propped a leaning, freshly puckered Billy Strum from falling too. The Horvath twins quit arguing, and I ducked down lower trying to hide behind the horses' legs.

Pretty quick, I didn't have anywhere to hide. At the teacher's yell, Cross's flightly mare had spooked and jumped sideways away from me. After she pulled away, the other five horses jerked their reins from my grip and ran off too – leaving me hunkered down and right out in the open.

Cross and Philmore and the Horvath twins took advantage of the diversion and ran after their horses. Dessie gave Billy Strum a push up, and he ran off too. But before I could get away, Miss Quail stepped over and grabbed my overalls. She glared down at the fallen girls. They stood and followed as the teacher scuttled me up the hill and into the hot-house school room, right up front to her desk. Miss Quail jerked open her top right drawer and hauled out her thick leather strap.

I didn't figure it was fair that I should be getting a licking when I hadn't done anything, and I said so. They didn't hang the kid that held Jesse James's horses, did they?

Miss Quail wouldn't believe me, though. She pulled my right hand out, sweaty palm up and her arm was rising for the first whack when Dessie piped up and said that I hadn't done anything. Miss Quail kept her arm raised though, as she waited for her pet student to speak. Patsy was still whoozy from her fall, but she straightened her glasses, leaned over close and peered at me (I suppose I must've looked a bit like Philmore). When she saw it was me, Patsy shook her head and said, "Nope, that one didn't kiss me."

I let out a big sigh and quit wincing as Miss Quail slowly lowered her arm. She stood with the limp strap dangling. Finally, she nodded her head toward the door and we three scuttled out of the stifling hot room.

When we got outside, Dessie and Patsy split off and ran over to where the other girls were skipping rope.

As I angled over to the boys' side, it dawned on me that I was the oldest boy left on the schoolgrounds. I slowed to a walk, tucked a thumb behind each overall strap, and strolled over to where my little brother Ferris and his friends were shooting marbles. I pretended to study a game of potsies while sneaking looks at the other side of the playground.

The younger girls had all crowded around Patsy and Dessie. Patsy whispered something, then touched Dessie's blushing cheek. The girls' eyes opened wide. But when Patsy grinned and pressed two fingers against her lips, the other girls' mouths shaped "OOOHs." My little sister, Clara, she giggled and pointed towards me. The others turned to look at me too.

Emeline didn't "oooh" or giggle. She crossed her arms and glared at me – her eyes blazing bright as a blacksmith's forge. Dessie noticed. She touched Emeline's shoulder and whispered something in her ear. Quick as I can speak it, the brimfire settled to a cosy glow, and Emeline gave me a relieved smile. I grinned back at her . . . and at Dessie.

Dessie Nordmark saved my bacon twice that morning. Thinking on that almost made up for not getting to kiss her.

I guess after the horses had pulled away from me, they'd galloped all the way down the road to our place. By the time the boys caught them, and rode the mile and a half back to school, Miss Quail had calmed down some. She gave the boys a tongue-lashing instead of the expected strap.

My dog had trailed Philmore and the rest back to the schoolhouse. Caleb did follow me to school once in a while, but Miss Quail always made me send him home. That day though, she must have been feeling guilty about my near strapping, because she said Caleb could stay. She even said he could join our afternoon jaunt.

After us boys put our horses back in the school pasture, Miss Quail asked Cross if there were any cattle – especially bulls – out on pasture yet. Cross said no, he didn't figure his dad had anything out on range yet.

Bulls were about the only thing in the world that Miss Quail was afraid of, although you could probably say that she was scared of any type of cow-critter. Miss Quail was raised in the city and until somebody proved different, she considered anything with four legs and a switch tail to be a bull.

After Cross jerked open the range-fence gate, Miss Quail made us boys stand aside while the girls filed through the gate first. For a ways, we boys stayed behind, in double file marching order, until Caleb ran ahead after a squeaking gopher and we ran off to help him. The zig-zag chase ended when the gopher skipped down a hole just below the slope of the first of the Buffalo Hills. Caleb jabbed his nose down the hole, then started to dig, until another gopher squeaked halfway up the hill.

Now I'm not sure whether the hills got their name from the herds that used to roam there, or from the fact that the hills rolled along one after the other like a herd of buffalo humps. The dun-brown hills were in the process of changing to their spring colors. Skinny green blades poked like Porcupine quills through the old dry grass, and clumps of purple-petalled, yellow-centred crocuses sprouted over the south-facing slopes.

As we boys ran up the first grassy ridge, a V-shaped flock of Canada geese passed overhead heading north. They flew so low we could easy hear the "whoosh . . . whoosh . . . whoosh" of slow-flapped wings and the gabbled gossip of the V-line's tail-enders.

After travelling a half mile, we topped a hill and looked down on a half acre slough. We boys ran down towards the water. We were met by the "kil-dee, kil-dee-dee" of a frightened killdeer. We got closer and the red-eyed mother bird got real worried and tried to lure us away from her nest by running past "kil-dee-deeing" and dragging a "crippled" right wing.

While the other boys were looking for its nest, I wrapped my arms around Caleb's neck to keep him from chasing the bird. By the time the girls and Miss Quail wandered down the hill, Philmore had found the nest. He and Cross stood spread-legged over it, keeping everybody else back so's they wouldn't step on it. Philmore, he reached down and picked up a blotchy brown and black egg. He lifted it, then held it out and showed the egg round the circle so's all us boys could see and touch it. We backed off so a circle of girls could have a look too. The mother killdeer fluttered just out of reach, all the time squawking, "Kil-dee, kil-dee-dee-dee." But she didn't make any complaint compared to Miss Quail. Once she saw what was going on, our teacher pushed through the circle of girls and snatched the egg away from Philmore. "Don't you boys know anything about wild birds?" she shouted into Philmore's face. Both he and Cross stepped back away from the nest.

Miss Quail motioned towards the mother bird with the egg. "She won't take it back you know, this egg," she said, waving it in the two boys faces. Leaning down and setting the egg on the grass, Miss Quail said, "There is no point contaminating the other three eggs." Miss Quail said as she set the egg on the grass. She frowned at the boys. "You did not touch any of the others did you?" In unison, the boys shook their heads no.

"Let this be a lesson to you, to you all," she said as she lifted her right foot.

Emeline had walked over close to Caleb and me while all this was going on. She kicked the grass as Miss Quail spoke, turned away and moaned, "Oh no!" as the teacher's foot came down with a thump, and a faint crushing sound.

Miss Quail lifted her foot. Underneath there were bits of shell scattered around a yellow-orange stain on the grass. Caleb and me turned away to watch a green-headed mallard and his plain-Jane mate swim to the far side of the slough and wriggle in amongst the cattails.

Miss Quail scraped the bottom of her shoe on the grass and carried on up the hill. The rest of us kids trailed after her. For a few minutes, us boys were a much more subdued group.

It didn't appear that Miss Quail believed Cross about the absence of bulls. At the top of the next couple hills, she shaded her eyes with a flat palm and scouted all four horizons. After a while, we boys livened up again and took the lead. Miss Quail, she got quieter and dropped back to listen to the girls' chatter.

The chinook wind gusted harder again. It strained and tugged at the clumps of crocuses, exposing their fuzzy stems and flapping their purple petals against the old grass.

What with the girls stopping to stoop and pick bunch after bunch of crocuses, us boys were one full ridge ahead when we sighted our destination. The rocky hub of the Medicine Wheel sat perched atop the highest spot in the Buffalo Hills. Close to thirty rocky spokes shot from the hub out to its circling rim of rocks.

We raced up that hill, hopped over the outside rim and ran along one of the rocky spokes to the big cairn at the wheel's hub.

When I say there was a big pile of rocks in the Medicine Wheel's hub, I mean big – thousands of rabbit to badger-sized rocks piled six feet high and thirty feet across. Us farm boys sure could appreciate the amount of picking and packing it took to accumulate a pile like that.

Grass sprouted in the blow sand that had filled the cracks between the bottom layers of rocks. You could tell the pile had been stacked a long time because lots of black moss was stuck to the rocks, even on the sunny side.

Cross Harmon touched and stroked the moss-fuzzy stones like they were something special to him.

The rest of us got to groping and poking our fingers into the crevices grubbing for hidden treasures. Caleb, he snuffled alongside me as I kneeled down close to the base to check the prickly grass for arrowheads. We only found a couple broken points, before Philmore and Billy and some others scrambled onto the hub. I boosted Caleb up top, then crawled after him.

Standing on our windy perch, we could see all the way south to the elevator row in Vulcan. Turning right, we followed the distant, jagged edge of the Rocky Mountains as it curved across the westen horizon, a hand's width under the chinook clouds' broad arch. To the north of us was Calgary, I guess, but you couldn't see it for the rolling hills. To the east, past our school-house and past Snake Valley's three white grain elevators, sprawled the wide open spaces of the Blackfoot Indian Reservation.

It was the Indians, Cross's grandmother's people, who'd built the Medicine Wheel. While Philmore and Billy and the Horvaths clumped over the rocks chanting, "Pow, wow wow," I wondered whether the Indians would have had buffalo-hide teepees poking up all around the base of the hill, with drums pounding rhythm for high-stepping dancers. Looking down at Cross as he sorted amongst the bones and rocks, I figured it was more likely the hill was a quiet spot where Medicine Men went to listen to Manitou – probably at night, with the velvet-black sky above, prickly with stars.

I'd asked Rufus Poor Eagle once what the Medicine Wheel was for. Rufus was Cross's great uncle, and me and him were pretty good friends. But the old chief wrinkled his brow, shook his head and said he didn't figure he ought to tell Blackfoot secrets to a white kid. I've got to admit I was pretty disappoint-ed, but I know Rufus told Cross some of the old Indian secrets before he died.

When Miss Quail walked over the hill and saw where we were, she yelled at us to get down off the rockpile. She got madder and louder as she got close enough to see that somebody, not us, had kicked a lot of the wheel's rim and spoke stones out of place. Some of the stones had been reset to spell out folks' initials: H.R.J., and P.M.+P.H. inside a heart. Cross was already moving rocks back in place when Miss Quail got there, and she put us all to work resetting the scattered spoke and rim stones.

As I hefted and reset a dozen rocks, there was a tingly feeling running up and down my spine that might have been mystical, but most likely was the result of working head to head with a smiling Dessie Nordmark. Dessie was upwind of me. Each time she stooped, stray wisps of her long, blond hair flicked against my cheeks and nose – along with whiffs of coal oil.

When Emeline found a clay doll while she was sorting rocks, Miss Quail got real excited. She lifted the big-bellied doll for all of us to see. It looked ugly to me, but our teacher said that it was a very unusual find and should be shown to an archeaologist, but when she fingered it and looked at it closer, Miss Quail decided the doll wasn't very old after all and gave it back to Emeline.

Miss Quail had taken a course on Blackfoot Indians during the summer. She said that the Blackfoot had sacred ceremonies up on the hill, and that they probably sacrificed there. That wasn't too hard to guess seeing as there were a fair number of bones scattered around – from tiny little bird and rabbit bones on up to hefty buffalo and elk thigh bones. Pointing out some good-sized rocks with swirly, red-stained fossil marks on them, Miss Quail said that they represented buffalo to the Indians. The Blackfoot offered these buffalo stones along with other gifts to the great Manitou so he'd make the herds multiply and be easier to find.

"Like this," Miss Quail said as she took a fossil rock from Cross and set it onto the hub-cairn. Cross set a leg bone beside it.

The girls decided to leave an offering too. They stuffed bunches of crocuses into Miss Quail's arms, and she lifted the flowers and set them on top of the cairn. The chinook had died considerably by then. The breeze ruffled the purple petals, but didn't blow the bunches off.

For almost a week Cross had been whittling a heavy chunk of willow stick. He'd tucked it into his pocket whenever anybody got close. I did sneak a good look one time though, so I've got my suspicions as to who it was supposed to be – she wore glasses. Anyway, after watching the girls offer their crocuses, Cross pulled the willow stick from his pocket and nestled it in amongst the flowers. Emeline, she smiled at me and asked Miss Quail to set her clay doll up top too.

Before we left, a meadowlark landed on the hub-cairn and hopped over the rocks. When it got to the flowers it puffed out its speckled, yellow chest and treated us to a lilting serenade. Meadowlarks may not be the snappiest dressers, but they sure can sing.

On the way back, our teacher was definitely feeling better. She scolded us boys for running ahead after Caleb, and made us walk close and in pairs while she talked about Indian lore and explained how millions of buffalo used to roam the prairies. She knelt down with Cross and they showed us how the new grass was almost ready for grazing. Cross had got interested enough to show us all how the old prairie wool grass always lays pointing South-East. He said that was how Indians who were lost in a storm could tell which way was which.

Miss Quail got so enthused about Cross joining in that she forgot to scout for cattle at the top of each rise.

Turned out she should've kept looking. After we'd travelled about a mile, a herd of cattle came tumbling over the nearest ridge to the south of us. Cross Harmon's dad must've just let his yearling steers out of their winter's pasture – the white-faced devils were bucking and kicking and running like a bunch of school's-out-for-summer kids.

When Philmore shouted, "Look at them cattle!" Miss Quail's head snapped to the right, her jaw dropped, and she stopped walking. She grabbed hold of Patsy Miller's shoulders and pulled the girl into her chest. Patsy was surprised because she hadn't seen the cattle yet. She tipped her head back and side-ways to look up at Miss Quail. Patsy's glasses weren't meant to be worn upside down and they tumbled into the prairie grass, but Miss Quail wouldn't let the girl loose to retrieve them.

Caleb had been busy sniffing for gophers out ahead of us when the running cattle spotted him. The lead steers bellered and angled his way. The rest of the herd followed. Caleb spun around. He perked his ears toward the cattle, then he turned tail and ran straight towards us kids.

When she saw my chicken dog heading our way, and the cattle sighting in on him, Miss Quail reached her arms out and pulled a couple more kids against Patsy and her. After they were in place, she reached out and grabbed another pair, and then another. Most of the girls and the little boys were watching the cattle with wide-open mouths and backing toward our teacher anyway. Pretty soon, Miss Quail was at the peak of her very own kid triangle.

Billy Strum and the Horvath twins knew a good thing when they saw it; they stepped behind Miss Quail.

That group of humans must have looked inviting to a scared dog. Ignoring the girls' squeals, Caleb ducked under their trembling skirts and scuffled on his belly into the middle of Miss Quail's scrum.

Even though their initial target had disappeared, the cattle didn't slow up and continued racing towards us kids. Philmore and Cross looked at one another and stepped away from the group to face the steers.

I wasn't sure what to do: step up with the big boys or join the Horvaths, when someone ran up against me. It was a girl, and when she wrapped her arms around me, I couldn't have moved if I'd wanted to. I figured it must be Emeline, but after sniffing a scent of coal oil, I looked down to see Dessie Nordmark's blue eyes gazing up at me! She flashed me a worried smile and my knees gave way. Dessie had to hug me even tighter to keep me standing.

Once I got over the shock, I glanced around to see where Emeline was.

She wasn't amongst Miss Quail's trembling group or with the gawking Horvaths. Was I ever surprised to see that she'd stepped up to join Cross and Philmore where they faced the stampeding cattle!

When the steers were almost on top of them, Philmore and Cross swept off their cloth caps and waved them and shouted. Emeline untied her white bonnet and twirled it above her bristle-haired head. She out-waved and out-yelled the bonnet-ducking boys.

The lead steers bobbed their heads and kicked as they shied away from our three brave ones. The herd parted like a white-faced red sea and two ground-trembling waves swept by on either side of us.

The bucking, kicking herd re-formed behind us, then circled around and headed back for another run at us. Cross, Philmore and Emeline turned left and stepped out front to meet the rush again. Miss Quail sidestepped around too, keeping her triangle's wide base pointing towards the steers. When the triangle moved, Caleb was out in the open, but only for a second before he scrambled back under his skirt cover. Me and Dessie and the Horvaths all turned to watch the cattle too.

This time, the oncoming steers broadened into a running half-moon, with the corners pointing forward. Before they reached us, the herd slowed and skittered to a snorting, blowing stop. The centre steers stood only a few yards in front of Cross, Philmore and Emeline. Our protectors stopped yelling and waving, but they stood firm. The whole herd stared at them. The steers obviously weren't used to getting so much exercise. Most of them had their pink tongues lolled out, and they were huffing and puffing.

Except for the steers' heavy breathing, everything was quiet, and everyone held their positions. Our brave three stood shoulder, to crew-cut head, to shoulder. Me and Dessie cuddled closer, but didn't move. A quiver ran down the centre of Miss Quail's triangle until a skirt lifted at the base as Caleb poked his head out.

A couple of the front steers jumped back. That spooked the rest. The whole herd turned tail and rumbled in a red-rumped wave over the hill, headed toward the Medicine Wheel.

Everybody stayed put for a good minute. It probably felt more like a half hour to the trembling Miss Quail. But to me, wrapped in the arms of a warm-blooded girl, it didn't seem nearly long enough. When one of the Horvath twins gawked around and saw me and Dessie together, he punched his brother in the shoulder and they started arguing. Their squabble broke the spell for everybody else.

Dessie loosened her grip and I sucked in the first breath I'd taken for a couple minutes. I sighed it out again after Dessie whispered, "Thank you," and kissed me.

My cheeks heated up like twin hotplates and my guts tightened in spots I'd never noticed before. I watched Dessie step over and drop to her knees beside Patsy to help her friend look for her fallen glasses.

I was still staring when Emeline grabbed me by the shoulder, spun me around and asked me who the heck I was looking at.

"It's me who stood up to those crazy cattle," she said.

I inhaled, then sighed, "Yeah that was something, wasn't it?"

As Emeline marched me away, I was still gazing over my shoulder at Dessie.

Once the steers were gone, Miss Quail's protective triangle (Caleb and all) faded away too, and our teacher stood in a glassy-eyed daze all alone, except for Patsy and Dessie who were searching the grass around her feet. After Dessie found the glasses, we headed back to school with Cross and Philmore each cradling one of Miss Quail's arms. They led our stumbling, mumbling teacher all the way back to the range-fence gate.

One of the Horvath twins was opening the gate when the Harmon steers tumbled over the hill, headed toward us again. Cross and Philmore let go of Miss Quail. They ran out with Emeline waving and shouting, and the steers angled down the fence away from us.

Miss Quail turned slowly when she heard the cattle coming. Her eyes widened at the sight of those white-faced red devils. She said, "Good Lord Jesus why?" and stood open-mouthed for a moment, then spun around, hopped over the fence and raced up to the schoolhouse – with Caleb no more'n two steps in front of her all the way. Us kids gawked in wonder and amazement. It was only a three wire fence, but Miss Quail had cleared the top wire without catching a single barb on her ankle-long skirt.

Although us kids didn't rub it in, Miss Quail never did get over that day's fright and embarrassment. Cross and Philmore left in May when the spring work started, but even with less kids to worry about, she just sort of sleep-walked through the rest of the school year. During the summer holidays Miss Quail married her bank teller boyfriend from Vulcan – an older fellow – and never come back to teach us.

Now that I've been around cattle for fifty odd years, I know that those steers were just feeling spunky and curious about our odd assortment of humans. Although they might've run over a kid by mistake, they sure wouldn't have hurt us on purpose.

But nobody in our school group, especially Miss Quail, knew it wasn't such a dangerous situation. I'd bet that our old teacher, wherever she is now, still figures that Cross and Philmore and Emeline are about the bravest kids she ever taught. Then again, she might be right.

Old Tom

"Wow," said Patti, "Grandma sure was brave."

"Our Mommy and Daddy have got cows, lots of big cows," Katie declared, "I wouldn't have been so scared as you Grandpa."

"I'll just bet you wouldn't either – neither one of you, " I said, rubbing both girls' bright red hair. "But you know, there are a few animals that a fellow, or young lady, should be spooked of."

❀ ❀ ❀

Old Tom was only a couple years younger than me, so you might say that we grew up together. But when I was fifteen, and just an unknown farm kid, Old Tom, at twelve, was already a Snake Valley legend.

Considering his origins, it's no wonder Old Tom ended up being a famous outlaw. Tom's mother, Babe, was an ornery Clydesdale mare who was forever causing Fussy Warner grief. Babe's working career ended one crispy-cool spring morning when she ran away with Fussy's stoneboat. The ornery mare dragged the stoneboat through a couple of page wire fences and ended up straddling the top rail of Fussy's corral fence like an equine teeter-totter. In her struggle to get back to earth Babe smashed the rails to splinters and crippled one of her hind legs.

Instead of shipping the troublemaker to the fox farm, Fussy sent her to the Buffalo Hills as a brood mare. The next spring

Babe birthed a scrawny, blood-bay colt. Since he was too light-boned to have been sired by one of the workhorse studs, the local wags figured Tom's daddy had to be a renegade cayuse from the Blackfoot Reservation – not an unlikely choice of beaus for a mare like Babe.

Late that fall Fussy corralled mother and son, so the local knife man could make a horse eunuch out of Tom. This upset Babe to no end. She crashed through the corral gate and led her blood-dripping son back out to the Buffalo Hills where they joined with a wild bunch of broomtails. That winter of 1919 was a tough one. It would've been hard for the crippled mare to rustle up enough grub for herself, let alone for her and a suckling colt. Babe didn't make it. Fussy found her in the spring. She hadn't been dead long because little Tom and the broomies were still hanging around the carcass trying to keep the coyotes off it (most likely the cause of Tom's strong dislike of all canines).

Fussy Warner felt sorry for the little orphan. After making a couple unsuccessful attempts to round Tom up, Fussy just let him run wild with the broomtail bunch. Tom grew up quick and tough, and within a couple years he had kicked and squealed and bit his way into the wild band's lead position.

Eventually Tom developed a reputation outside his broomtail band. Coyotes travelling through the Buffalo Hills were continually checking over their shoulders for a bad-tempered, bay gelding who always gave them a run for their money. Tom only occasionally took a run at riders but a story made the rounds claiming that Babe's wild-eyed, wide-nostrilled son could snort a man's hat off at under twenty feet. In another year or two the rumors had him snorting hats off at thirty feet, then forty, then on up to fifty feet. Tom's twin blowers appeared to be getting stronger with age and with practice. Human travellers as well as canines started giving Tom and his broomies a wide birth.

It was during the spring of Tom's twelfth year that the well known horsebreaker, H. J. MacInnes, placed an ad in the local paper saying he planned on conducting a two day horse-training clinic in our area.

The advance billing took up an entire page in the May 12th edition of the *Snake Valley Slither*. Big black letters across the top of the page bragged:

THE HORSE HAS NOT BEEN BORN THAT
H. J. MACINNES CANNOT TAME.

Big plain letters farther down declared:

MACINNES DESIRES THE ROUGHEST,
TOUGHEST OUTLAW IN THE COUNTRY
UPON WHICH TO DISPLAY THESE
REMARKABLE SKILLS.

In small print near the bottom of the page was:

*The modest fee for partaking in this once in a
lifetime opportunity will be $15 per family (no limit
as to number, age, or sexual persuasion of family
members).*

There was no doubt as to what horse was Snake Valley's roughest, toughest outlaw. Old Tom won hands down. But there was some doubt as to whether any Snake Valley families could rustle up the "modest" fifteen dollar fee. Heck, that was half a months wages. Fifteen dollars would buy ten pairs of stiff new GWG bluejeans, or twenty-five restaurant meals – pretty pricey for two days of watching and talking horses.

My Pa figured that since our family was a bit better off than most, that we could afford to sign up for the clinic.

My Mother finally agreed, but only if Pa promised not to disturb the precious bank account. Pa looked pretty upset when he emptied his pockets and only found three dollars and seventy-eight cents, and some worthless pocket fuzz.

Mother shook her head, and pulled her egg-and-cream-money coffee tin down from the cupboard. She dumped a clattering pile of change and crumpled dollar bills onto the kitchen table. After sorting all the quarters and dimes and nickles, and even a couple piles of pennies, over with the dollar bills, she collected the fifteen dollars. It was close though. When she set the coffee tin back in the cupboard there were only a few coins left rattling inside.

A lot more of the same was going on all over Snake Valley that week, as other families cleaned out their own nest eggs. The ad said that it was fifteen dollars with "no limit on the number of family members." Interested parties extended out to half-uncles-in-law to gather the necessary cash for one "family" to attend the clinic.

Bill Hewitt, the farm manager at the Blackfoot Reserve paid thirty dollars: fifteen for the white folks on salary (they were all Bill's family), and fifteen more for the red folks.

The local wags scoffed and said that a fellow like Bill, spending government money, could *afford* to be extravagant. They figured Bill should've been able to sign up whites and reds for just fifteen dollars. Wasn't his cousin Hank married to Clara Weaselhead? Didn't all one hundred and sixteen of the folks on the Last Hill Hutterite Colony sign up for just fifteen dollars?

The ad in the paper had said that the family that owned the outlaw equine student would receive its tutoring "absolutely free of charge." That meant Fussy Warner didn't have to worry about digging up the money. The kicker was that as well as supplying the prize student (which H. J. MacInnes got to keep) the outlaw's owner was expected to supply H. J.'s room and board plus the training facilities.

That still meant Fussy would get to see the show for next to nothing. As far as most folks were concerned neither Old Tom, nor Fussy's facilities were worth spit.

What was Fussy's house like? Well, it would have taken considerable patching before that two storey shack would've held grain again. Fussy's white cat, Pearl, could slip in or out in a half-dozen different spots, not counting windows and doors.

Not that Pearl had much need for going outside. She birthed her bi-monthly batch of kittens right on top of Fussy's bed-spread; and a couple floorboards in the bedroom were broke away so Pearl and her little ones could use the dirt underneath as a litter box. A fellow with plugged up nostrils just had to step through Fussy's front door to clear his system all the way to his sinuses.

And Fussy's corrals? Well for the time being everybody that signed their names on the list, including my Pa, kept the cash safe in their pockets. On account of they weren't going to plunk down any hard-won coins and bills before Old Tom was safely ensconced in Fussy Warner's yard.

The crucial word there was "safely." Fussy's corrals were so flimsy that they'd have had trouble standing up to a baby's sneeze let alone to one of Old Tom's hurricane snorts. The old fellow still hadn't more than rough patched the fences and corral that Tom's mom busted a dozen years earlier.

The weekend before H. J. MacInnes was scheduled to arrive, Snake Valley held a fence-fixing bee at Fussy Warner's. While Fussy and Pearl were diverted by the digging and hammering and sawing going on over at the corrals, the local ladies supervised a shake down of Fussy's shack.

With clothes' pegs clamped on our noses, and scoop shovels in our hands us boys scraped and shoveled the empty tomato cans, curled-up potato peels and loose garbage out into the yard. We buried everything in a couple gopher holes that Caleb had kindly expanded for us.

We boys used spades, rakes and a big sieve to clean up Pearl's under-the-bedroom litter box. After we finished the ladies bustled in – also sporting clothes-pegged noses. They went to work washing the walls, windows and floors with buckets full of soapy water. Meanwhile our local handyman, Harvey Rudson, patched the half dozen cat holes plus a bunch more mouse-sized openings.

Following orders from the ladies, Caleb and us kids trans-ferred Pearl's latest batch of kittens – four white, three black and one pinto – from Fussy's bedspread down onto the clean, raked dirt beneath the floorboards (where Pearl could still get at them from under the porch step). As a finishing touch, Harvey Rudson tacked a couple shingles over top of the mewling hole.

In the meantime the menfolk had rebuilt Fussy's big, egg-shaped corral so that it stood high and solid as a pine-planked Maginot line. The local wags figured it was strong enough to pen in a herd of stampeding buffalo, and that it might even hold Old Tom.

When the men clumped over from the corral to the house, Fussy led the parade, puffing both his pipe and his chest. He and his white cat were sporting mile-wide Cheshire grins. Caleb and us kids and the women stood out of the way, wondering what Fussy would say about our cleaning job.

He didn't even notice the sparkling clean windows, but when Fussy opened the front door his jaw dropped – and so did his smoking pipe. Fussy's mouth hung wide open but no words of praise, no words of any kind came out – just a long drawn out, "ahhhhhh."

Pearl, though, she made enough racket for the both of them. That white cat howled like a banshee, her ridge hairs rose, her claws twanged out and she hooked into the shack.

Yowling all the while, Pearl clambered up and down and around the walls searching for her babies. Eventually we heard her ripping and tearing at Harvey's shingle patches. It was only three or four minutes between the time "hurricane Pearl" entered the house, to when she lay purring on the bedspread with her kittens attached; but that thin slice of time made one heck of a difference.

Fussy, he recovered his pipe, walked inside and looked around. There were pots and pans and shreds of wallpaper and wood splinters scattered everywhere. The old fellow nodded his head. Fussy appeared pleased with Pearl's renovations. He picked up a blue galvanized coffee pot, filled it at the stove and had it boiling and burping in no time.

The clean up had done some good though. Before the coffee aroma filled the room, Fussy's nose kept sniffing and twitching at the unfamiliar clean smell of lye soap.

Pearl must have noticed an unusual scent too – of dog – on her nursing kittens. When she'd filled her little ones' bellies Pearl sneaked outside and climbed up onto the porch roof. After coffee, when Caleb stepped out the door, Pearl pounced onto his back. That spiteful cat spurred my "kai-yaying" hound all the way to the road before retracting her claws and hopping off.

Fussy, though, he didn't hold a grudge. He never did make mention to Harvey or the ladies, or even to us kids about our meddling with his shack. But he sure did rave about his new corral; and since it was spruced up, the next order of the day was persuading Old Tom to come on over for a visit.

Fussy and Pa and the others set to forming a Snake Valley posse to round the outlaw up. They decided to push Old Tom and his broomtails in with the herd of tame horses that was still roaming the Buffalo Hills. They figured a roundup crew would have a good chance of chasing the mixed bunch in.

Seeing as I'd been out of school for almost a year, I hoped to be part of the roundup crew. I knew that my older brother Philmore and his best friend Cross Harmon would get to go, and my little brother Ferris, who was the baby of the family and a tad spoilt, he didn't have any doubt that he would be invited. After all, Pa'd just bought him a new pony.

Lucky for me Ferris was right. His going meant Pa couldn't very well say no to me. But Pa insisted that if we were coming, we'd both have to stay right behind him or Fussy, all the time. We hoped we'd be with Pa, because he'd be sure to be in the thick of things.

Friday, May 21, the day before H. J. MacInnes' clinic was to start, was the date set for Old Tom's roundup. We got up early and finished our chores before coming back in to eat. After breakfast, when we left the house, the eastern horizon glowed pink and yellow ahead of the morning sun.

Philmore had serviced and fueled his Model-T the night before. He just had to crank it up before he and Caleb jumped in and struck out for the Buffalo Hills to do some advance scouting. When Philmore wheeled past the barn, Caleb and him didn't even glance at us low-class, horse folk. Sitting up stiff and proud in their seats, and gazing straight ahead, those two looked like a cocky pair of parading princes.

Me and Ferris mounted and followed Pa's fast-walking grey over to Fussy's place where we met up with the rest of the roundup crew. Everybody rode out together, with Pa and Fussy up front.

Pa figured we'd best all keep to a walk, so as not to tire our horses out early. But his grey walked so fast that Fussy's pudgy little mare had to trot half the time to keep up. Me and Ferris were the back pair, and both riding bareback. Although my mare did alternate between walking and trotting, Ferris's pony had to trot all the time. Ferris's little round head bobbed up and down in rhythm with his little round backside. But he wasn't complaining. Ferris was pleased to be coming along, and kept on a-smiling, just as if he was in his right mind.

By the time we got to the pasture gate, the sun was warming our backs and lighting the yellow-brown humps of the Buffalo Hills. The tame workhorses were all gathered close by the fence picking the short green grass there.

Those big characters were awful disappointed when, instead of letting them out so they could come home, we headed them deeper into the hills to find Old Tom's wild bunch. The horses kept slowing down and swinging their big shaggy heads back to see if we were sure we wanted to go that way. Me and Ferris trailed a safe distance behind while Fussy and the other fellows on drag twirled their lariats and smacked the reluctant travellers' rumps.

We'd only proceeded a mile or so when I heard an engine roaring and saw dust billowing ahead. Next thing I knew Philmore's Model-T was silhouetted above the nearest hill – with all four tires in the air – just before it came a-ripping down at us in a tire-whumping hurry. Fifty feet back was Caleb, and right behind him was Old Tom at the head of his bunch of broomtails. Tom's head was lowered and his bared teeth were snapping at my dog's heels.

Pa and Cross Harmon had been riding the points. They yelled for Fussy and us tail enders to get the hell out of the way. Me and Ferris and the rest whipped our mounts over to the north side of the tame horse herd. Philmore swerved his car right and varoomed past the south side.

Caleb was running with his tail tucked between his legs and his head swung back over his left shoulder. He wasn't looking where he was going. With the "wildies" right behind him, Caleb ran smack dab into the middle of our tame herd. The two bunches collided. Horses reared and squealed, swapped ends and kicked and bit at one another.

I sighed with relief when Caleb tore out of that snarly knot of horseflesh. My dog's tail was still tucked but he wasn't looking back any more. That touch of greyhound blood was just a-racing through his veins as he flattened out, his pointy nose aimed straight at the Model-T's trunk. Unfortunately Old Tom had threaded the needle too. His front feet were flashing and flailing right behind my dog.

A thin line of misfits strung behind Caleb and Old Tom. Behind them lumbered the main bunch of tame horses with us riders "yippy-kai-yaying" at them to keep up. As they ran up one hillside and tumbled down the next, that ball of tame horses ebbed back and forth like a yo-yo on a wild horse string.

When our cavalcade hit the road, Pa and Cross Harmon raced their horses up along either ditch. They had to beat the leaders to Fussy's place. The rest of us were left in the rear ducking and dodging the dirt lumps hucked back by big, plate-sized hooves.

When Philmore got to Fussy's turnoff, he whipped the Model-T off into the driveway. Caleb and Old Tom turned too. They followed the car through Fussy's yard right into the big oval corral. Philmore braked and the dog and horse swished past him. Caleb scrabbled out under a bottom plank just ahead of Tom's flailing front feet. But before Philmore could shift into reverse, Pa slammed the corral gate shut. Philmore and his car were trapped inside with Old Tom as Cross and Pa directed the rest of the misfits into a page wire holding pen.

Me and Ferris trotted into the yard to the sound of explosive snorts and thumps. Old Tom was testing for weak spots down at the far end of the corral. Tom wasn't crazy enough to attack the fence head on. He'd snort, then hit the planks a glancing shoulder blow. After smacking the corral a couple dozen times without success, Tom started pawing dirt from under the bottom plank that Caleb had squeezed through.

When the outlaw started digging for freedom, Caleb got up, padded away from the fence and lay back down under the lee of the barn. He proceeded to pant and watch the proceedings from there.

Meanwhile Pa and Fussy were debating through the fence with Philmore about what to do with the Model-T. Philmore had backed his car over close to the corral gate, but the consensus was (Philmore being the only dissenter) that it wouldn't be smart to open the gate and take a chance on letting Old Tom escape. Philmore finally had to abandon his car, and climb up and over the plank fence.

After a few minutes Old Tom determined that a horse's hooves weren't suited to spade work. He stopped digging, snorted dirt and dust against the offending planks then turned and backed into the end of the corral. There he stood, with his bay head lowered, breathing heavy, glaring out at our cluster of men and riders.

For a few minutes everybody (except Philmore) sat atop their horses and marvelled at our good fortune. We were like a bunch of kids staring at a bay and black hornet we'd just trapped in a glass bottle. We didn't know exactly how we'd managed to catch him, and we didn't know what happened next (that was up to H. J. MacInnes), but there stood Old Tom – a Snake Valley legend – firmly ensconced in Fussy Warner's corral.

When everybody had finished marvelling, we cut out Fussy's horses and pushed the rest of the bunch onto the road. Philmore hopped on behind Cross and they rode double as we chased the horse herd to our place. My older brother wasn't happy to leave, he kept gazing back at his car. I heard Philmore tell Cross that he felt like a fellow leaving his best girl with a hairy-chested, licorice stick drummer. (Patsy Miller just loved licorice.)

My rear end felt a little the worse for wear after that long bareback ride, but when Ferris slipped down off his pony the little guy looked to be really hurting. On the way over to the house he was biting his lower lip and taking short choppy steps.

Turned out his rear-end was rubbed raw. He couldn't even eat, so our Mother salved his sores and put him to bed.

Pa had invited Fussy and Cross Harmon over for lunch. The afternoon's dinner discussion included a lot of across-the-table fork waving as those three debated the possibilities of Old Tom's slapping H. J. MacInnes around like a feeble-minded coyote. Philmore sat and scowled and didn't say anything. Caleb flopped down inside the door; him and me didn't take part in the speculations either.

After lunch everybody but sore-bottomed Ferris headed back over to Fussy's. Philmore rode my mare, and I had to dangle my long legs on either side of Ferris's jig-jogging pony.

Word travelled fast that we'd captured Snake Valley's equine legend and there were spectators galore gathered in Fussy's yard when we rode in. Old Tom still stood guard down at the far end of the corral. Now and again he would let go a wicked snort and lunge at the fence, sending the folks that'd crept too close scuttling away.

Philmore ignored a warning blast and ran over to the fence next to his Model-T. When he found his olive-green beauty intact and unsullied, Philmore sighed with relief. He reached his arm through the planks and brushed the dust off a big, wide-eyed headlight.

The local wags had deserted their chairs out in front of Marchand's Emporium, and come over to Fussy's for a look-see. They claimed that H. J. MacInnes arrived in town just before lunch. Those old seers proved to be dead right. About one-fifteen a fancy little roadster whirred down the road and ducked in Fussy's driveway.

The roadster's door opened and a high crowned, white stetson poked out. The door thunked shut, exposing the rest of the horsebreaker, and I almost burst out laughing. As he strutted towards the corral, H. J. MacInnes looked just like one of my Mother's white Banty roosters. The pint-sized cowboy wore feather-white pants stuffed inside high topped, white riding boots. His white satin shirt was trimmed with red swirls, and he had a puffy, red silk scarf wrapped around his neck.

The folks around me shook their heads, then smiled knowingly at one another. Kids pointed and covered their mouths so as not to snicker. The local wags were gape-mouthed. You could just see the odds shooting up to a hundred to one that this duded-up, penny arcade cowboy would ever best our equine champion.

The cocky cowboy kept striding towards the corral, not seeming to notice our looks of disbelief.

MacInnes noticed my particularly shocked look. He stopped, pointed a white-gloved finger at me and asked in a husky, deep voice, "You meaning to catch flies in that wide open trap of yours son?" Then he carried on.

Shoot! I always attract the wrong kind of attention.

Pa and Fussy were standing by the corral gate. Pa managed to keep a straight face as he swung the gate open for MacInnes. The horsebreaker nodded, then pranced into the corral. Pa stepped in too, but Fussy stayed outside. After the old fellow latched the gate shut, he crossed himself – and heck, Fussy's not even Catholic.

Caleb and me ran over to the fence to get a better view of the action.

MacInnes was strutting past Philmore's car when Old Tom let go with an eardrum blasting snort. But the horsebreaker kept walking until he was about a third of the way down the egg shaped corral, where he stopped, set a hand on either hip and stood studying Old Tom.

After letting go with his warning snort, Old Tom had backed against the far end corral planks. The outlaw's ears were jacked forward and his nostrils flared wide. His white-rimmed eyes fired darts to the right, to the left, then straight at MacInnes. But Tom appeared to be at a loss as to what to do next. It appeared certain, as flabbergasted as he looked, that the old devil hadn't ever faced a fancied-up horsebreaker before.

Pa walked over beside MacInnes. When the horsebreaker noticed that he had been favored with company, he started gabbing with Pa, occasionally jabbing a finger towards Tom to emphasize this or that point.

Each time the horsebreaker's hand shot out, Tom tensed and snorted. Each time I figured something had to happen. But both Pa's cloth cap and MacInnes' stetson stayed put – they didn't even flutter. I estimated the distance between men and beast as eighty feet and noted in my mental files: hats safe at eighty feet.

While Pa and MacInnes stood jawing in the middle of the corral, I checked out Old Tom's figure myself.

He wasn't huge, only about fifteen hundred pounds, but he was nicely put together. Tom had wide spaced eyes, a deep barrel chest and good straight legs ending with strong black hooves. A handy-sized specimen of a working horse to my youngster's eyes.

Back then we drove mostly good solid smaller horses on our working outfits. We didn't go in for those long-geared, high-stepping parade types that you see nowadays – pulling empty beer wagons up and down city streets.

When MacInnes and Pa had finished visiting, they turned and headed back towards the gate. Old Tom's ears perked when MacInnes motioned Pa to drive Philmore's Model-T outside. At first Pa shook his head no, but MacInnes insisted, so Pa cranked-started the engine then hurried back and hopped into the driver's seat. MacInnes swung the gate wide open. As Pa puttered the car outside, Old Tom's ears perked and he trotted forward too. At a knife-sharp glance from MacInnes, the outlaw stopped dead in his tracks, like a Suffolk ram froze by a sheep dog's stare.

MacInnes kept an eye on the horse while Philmore (he had to be dragged away from his car) and Cross Harmon set two buckets of water and a half-bale of prairie wool inside the corral. When they came back out, MacInnes shut the gate then he strutted over toward Fussy's house.

The local wags nodded their heads in grudging approval. You could see their rheumy eyes calculating the horsebreaker's odds back down to five or ten to one.

H. J. MacInnes, after surveying the accommodations he was going to have to share with Fussy and Pearl, decided to forego his claim on room and board. The horsebreaker climbed back into his roadster and headed to town to get a room at the Snake Valley Hotel.

The next morning we made it to Fussy's plenty early, but we barely had time to tie our horses before H. J. MacInnes wheeled his roadster into the yard.

A different looking horsebreaker stepped out of the car that morning. H. J. MacInnes was shod in dun-colored riding boots that were tucked inside a pair of well-worn blue jeans. He wore a loose-fitting, plaid work shirt and topped the outfit off with a beaver-brown stetson. As he sauntered past my dog and me, I caught a hint of perfume. H. J. must've noticed my sniffing, though. He didn't stop, but called over his shoulder, "You got a cold there flycatcher?"

"I've done it again!" I thought to myself as Caleb and me ran over to the corral. I climbed up the fence and sat on top; Caleb hunkered down to watch proceedings from under the bottom plank.

Down at the end of the corral, Old Tom was raising dust. He must've spent the entire night pacing back and forth like a caged cat, because his hooves had gouged a fist deep trail along the fence. The old outlaw didn't even stop to eat or drink – he hadn't touched his hay, and his water buckets were still brim full and skimmed with dust.

Although Tom's stomach may have been hanging slack, his lungs were in fine fettle. When H. J. MacInnes stepped into the corral Old Tom greeted the horsebreaker with a nostril flapping snort; then he backed against the fence, lowered his head and pawed dirt like a mad bull.

None of this fazed MacInnes. H. J. didn't even break stride, just kept strutting to the centre of the corral where he stopped and crossed his arms. H. J.'s right hand rose to cup his chin; two long, thin fingers tip-tapped his nose as he studied Tom.

Cross Harmon and Pa walked up and stood on either side of the tiny horsebreaker. H. J. was happy for the company. While he talked, MacInnes swung his arms this way and that, waving his hands like a full-blooded Frenchman – making Pa and Cross lean away from him to keep from getting swatted.

Old Tom glared with narrowing eyes at the hand-waving MacInnes. Tom sucked in deeper and deeper breaths. Finally, when his chest was gut wideningly full, the big horse discharged a humongous snort that puffed the dust fifteen feet in front of him. All three humans stopped talking and looked at Tom, but their headgear remained in place. "Hats safe at sixty feet."

Old Tom laid back his ears, bared his teeth and charged.

H. J. MacInnes didn't dodge or run. He just leaned forward and stared his sheepdog's stare at Tom. Pa's and Cross's boots stayed planted too, but their heads and bodies did tilt back, away from the oncoming outlaw. I leaned back myself, in sympathy, and almost tumbled off my perch.

When I levered myself back into a viewing position, Old Tom had skittered to a stop not more that six feet in front of MacInnes. The buffaloed horse let out a wimpy snort, turned tail and slunk back to his starting point.

The skidding outlaw had sprayed dirt all over MacInnes and Pa and Cross. After swatting their fronts clean, the men turned and strolled back towards the corral gate. They were all three chuckling. MacInnes' laugh reminded me of a girl's screechy giggle, and Pa and Cross were laughing higher pitched than normal too. They sounded like three kids who'd just barely squeaked out of a tight spot.

They left the corral and walked on over to MacInnes' roadster. Pa and Cross watched as H. J. sorted through his horsebreaking gear in the back.

Meanwhile a mixed bag of farmers' buggies and wagons and cars began trailing into Fussy's yard. Philmore's Model-T was one – chauffeuring our mother, three sisters and a pillow-sitting Ferris.

A long line of horse-drawn grain tanks rolled down from the west, from the First Hill Hutterite Colony. Sitting on the wagon seats were straight-backed, black-suited fellows. Grinning over the sides were black-capped boys mixed in with kerchiefed women and girls.

From the east came Bill Hewitt and his Blackfoot Indian Reserve crew. Bill led the way, driving a prancing team of black thoroughbreds on his democrat. Behind him trailed a few cars and buggies, but mostly a colorful band of Indian riders mounted on palominos, pintos and buckskins. The riders wore flashy colored cowboy shirts. The horses sported feathers in their manes and painted hand prints on their rumps.

Even Fussy's "commodious" yard (as the old fellow liked to refer to it) couldn't hold all the vehicles. The latecomers had to leave their outfits parked on the side of the road or down in the ditches. There were as many folks bustling around as you'd see on a Saturday afternoon at the annual Snake Valley race meet. The languages spoken ranged from the Hutterites' husky German, through sing-song Norwegian, to the soft lispings of the Blackfoot. Caleb and me and Ferris wandered amongst the crowd, Caleb sniffing noses with the dogs and us jabbering with the kids.

Unfortunately, Caleb and me and Ferris had got so wrapped up in the hustle and bustle that by the time we started looking for a place to watch the show, the corral was rimmed almost all the way around with shoulder to shoulder fence sitters. And under them stood a couple more rows of between-the-plank-peerers. It was actually quite a striking sight, with the cowboys and Blackfoot braves' orange and yellow and purple shirts scattered amongst clumps of Hutterite black, and the brown and blue of the dirt farmers. But Caleb and me and Ferris didn't have time to enjoy the view. We had to find a spot to watch the horse breaking.

The three of us ran back and forth behind the packed between-the-plank-peerers. Finally at the far end of the corral Caleb and me squeezed through an opening. I crawled up, wrapped my arms around the top of a fence post and peered through the hip gap left by two big shouldered cowboys. Caleb hunkered down and got a low angle shot from under the bottom plank. Ferris poked and prodded trying to get a viewing spot too but nobody would let him in.

I didn't have time to worry about my little brother's sight line, though, because H. J. MacInnes – all by his lonesome – was slowly approaching his quarry. He was holding a long bamboo binder whip out in front of him, just like he was toting a fishing pole. But, instead of dangling a fish-hook and line, that whip had a halter swinging from the end, with its shank rope running down the pole and into MacInnes' hands. The tail of the shank rope slithered behind him, leaving a twisty trail in the dust.

Old Tom had pressed his haunches hard against the far end of the groaning corral. He stood stiff and still as MacInnes walked towards him. There were no folks foolish enough to sit on the fence within thirty or forty feet of Tom, but from then on, all around either side, the corral was packed. Wide-eyed Tom kept swivelling his head from one side of the whispering crowd to the other with stops in between to check on the slowly approaching horsebreaker.

As MacInnes stepped closer, Old Tom's white-rimmed eyes got to watching the long bamboo pole. The horsebreaker spoke to Tom quiet and easy, like you would to a bad-tempered wife. H. J. swung the pole slowly in front of him from right to left, left to right, right to left. The horse watched as the halter swayed on the end of the pole, and his big bay head got to swaying back and forth, and watching the halter, and the people stopped whispering, and their heads started weaving back . . . and . . . forth and back . . . and . . . forth; and my head and shoulders started swaying in time with the fellows' above me as MacInnes eased closer and closer to a gently swaying Tom.

I guess my little brother Ferris couldn't stand the suspense any longer. He squeezed through the weaving crowd and started jumping up and down and beating the backs of my legs. In the process Ferris tromped on my dog's tail. Caleb yelped and squirted under the bottom rail, right into the middle of the corral!

The rim-crowd leaned forward and gasped a unanimous "Oooh-Noo!" and Old Tom stopped swaying. He shook his head then let go with a monstrous snort before diving after Caleb. Tom's snort neatly dislodged the horsebreaker's brown stetson. ("Not safe under 25 feet.") As the stetson tumbled backwards, brim over crown, I saw a chestnut-colored pony tail drop down the middle of H. J. MacInnes' back!

I don't suppose anyone else noticed. Most everybody was ducking and diving and generally getting out of the way as Old Tom charged around the outside of the corral after my dog. I hugged my post closer as the big-shouldered cowboys toppled backwards off the fence behind me and thumped onto the ground below. (It was darned lucky Caleb wasn't still lying there – those hefty characters would have flattened my dog like a Mexican pancake.)

With the fence cleared, Ferris climbed up beside me. I pointed to H. J. MacInnes, but it was too late. *She* was kneeling in the middle of the corral scrunching the high-crowned hat back onto her head. I tried to explain what I'd seen – but Ferris was too busy watching the horse and the dog to listen to my story.

I wasn't too worried about Caleb – he'd outrun Tom before. After my dog'd made one circuit of the oval, his pointy nose disappeared into the cloud of dust that had rolled up behind Old Tom. A second or two later Old Tom entered the cloud too. As the dust thickened and rose, the pursued and the pursuer gradually faded from sight.

Since there was no wind, that oval of grey-brown dust got to rising higher and higher and curling in on itself like a doughnut. The centre of the corral, and H. J. MacInnes, was just starting to dust up when the hoof thudding slowed.

Ferris shouted, "Look at that." And pointed as Old Tom staggered into the middle of the corral.

The strain of the roundup, combined with a night's pacing and now the running, had tuckered Old Tom out. His drooping ears perked though, when he sighted the still-circling Caleb in the dust. Old Tom didn't charge back into the fray though. His hind end sank to the ground and his outstretched front feet paddled him around and around so he could follow my dog's circuits.

By Caleb's fourth or fifth solo circuit, the dust was settling and Old Tom was getting dizzy. The big horse's eyes started to roll and after a couple more turns Tom toppled onto his side. H. J. MacInnes ran in quick and hooked Tom's head with the dangling halter.

Old Tom's collapse didn't happen any too soon for Caleb. My dog staggered over and plopped down beside his entry hole. Me and Ferris reached under the plank, grabbed his front paws and dragged him through. That poor dog felt about as limber as a wrung-out dishrag.

Meanwhile the top of the corral had re-rimmed with people, so me and Ferris had to lay down and peer under Caleb's plank.

A freshly haltered Old Tom, stood splay-legged and wobbly in the middle of the corral. The big horse didn't fight at all as MacInnes covered his still rolling eyes with a wide, black handkerchief. MacInnes stepped back from the blindfolded outlaw with her hands gripping the long shank. She signalled for Pa and Cross to come in and help.

Nobody clapped or anything (a couple of the local wags sighed) but we all knew that Old Tom had met his match.

Pa and Cross helped MacInnes tug Tom's head to one side then the other and back again. At first the big horse fought and struck and snorted. Pretty soon, though, they were easing him ahead a little with each crossways jerk. Within an hour Old Tom was stumbling behind MacInnes like a sightless Lear trailing his daughter.

In the afternoon H. J. set a foot stool on one side of the still blindfolded outlaw, then she invited a bunch of us young blades into the corral. H. J. had us kids run up, step onto the stool and vault over Tom's back like one of those pommel horses they've got in school gyms.

MacInnes told us to set two palms on the horse's back, push off and over. But I was feeling sorry for Old Tom. I gave him a reassuring pat on the neck as I went over. I sure shouldn't have!

Tom tensed and humped his back like he was about to explode. He sent me sailing through the air twice as far as anybody else.

After I'd picked myself up, H. J. fixed me with a glint-eyed stare. "You . . . Flycatcher," she said. "You'd best listen up son, or get the hell out of my corral."

After that chewing out, I had a pretty good idea why H. J. MacInnes was staring down wild horses instead of partaking in the joys of matrimonial bliss. Not that knowing she was a female meant I had any less respect for her. If anything, I had more respect for a woman horsebreaker. H. J. MacInnes couldn't have found herself a meeker, milder student after just one warning.

On Sunday even more folks turned up for the show (Caleb stayed home for a rest, though). By the afternoon Old Tom was harnessed and his blindfold was off and MacInnes was driving him around Fussy's yard paired with a trusty old horse of ours named Brownie. Tom still snorted and jumped once in a while, but by the end of the day he'd started to turn and stop and mind the bit pretty well.

It was lucky Caleb didn't come that day. After that evening's pot luck supper, Pa shocked everyone when he made out a twenty-five dollar cheque to H. J. MacInnes for Old Tom. We drove Brownie and Old Tom home to our place that night. Tom was to become a regular member of our workhorse crew.

There are lots of stories I could tell about working with the old devil, but the gist of it is, even though he was a willing worker, Tom never did lose his spunk. He was always ready for a good snort, or a run, if something upset him.

We'd had Tom for a couple years when Philmore talked Pa into making a deal for one of those new Hart-Parr tractors that were flooding the country. A half-dozen horses got thrown in on the deal. Old Tom was one of them.

The Hart-Parr dealer figured on shipping his trade horses up north, to the Peace River country where they still used a lot of workhorses. But Old Tom didn't appreciate being hauled by a hissing, puffing steam locomotive that could out-snort him. The railway's teamsters tugged and shoved and cussed Tom for over an hour – they tried every trick they knew but couldn't get him loaded.

Bill Hewitt happened to be in Snake Valley that day. When he offered five bucks for the old outlaw, the dealer threw in Tom's halter and shank with the bargain.

Bill Hewitt always did respect the old ways and the wild things. He didn't work Tom on the reserve farm. He sent Snake Valley's former equine hero to an early retirement out on the Blackfoot Reserve pasture.

The last year we spent in the Snake Valley country, Caleb and me were riding across that pasture when we ran across Old Tom and a bunch of his wild cousins. The old outlaw was slick and fat and sure looked pleased with the way life had turned out for him. Tom was feeling so good he gave Caleb a token snort, and half-mile run – just for old times sake.

Sunday Rodeo

This particular Sunday morning Reverand Smidke droned on so long about the evils of holding thine own self above the Lord, that we were late getting home. And then we had a devil of a time catching little brother Ferris's pony. By the time we fast-trotted into Clifford Medicine Shield's yard the rodeo action had already started.

A bronc's hooves pawed dust-puffs as it bucked and kicked and grunted across the arena. The would-be rider sailed off, his fork end up. But the grey kept bucking, and each time her front feet hit the ground the slack stirrups swung up above the empty saddle and clacked together.

My older brother Philmore shook his head. He turned to Cross Harmon. "That grey mare looks ranker than anything Clifford let us ride last week."

"Yeah," said Cross with a nod. "And she's quick. I'd like to try her," he tapped the surcingle tied behind his saddle, "under this bareback rigging."

Cross and Philmore reined their horses over to the holding pen. Caleb and me and brother Ferris trailed after them.

Clifford Medicine Shield was leaning over the corral watching his two sons herd the grey bronc into the stripping chute. Every Sunday during the summer Clifford gathered a bunch of half-wild cayuses off the Blackfoot reserve so that the young bucks of Snake Valley (both red and white) could try them out, and maybe even break a few.

Cross rode up behind Clifford. He leaned over and tapped the big Blackfoot chief on the shoulder. "Clifford," he said. "Do you think you could run that grey back in for me to try?"

The big man was surprised. He turned quickly. "Eh. What's that?" His eyes squinched shut, and he tipped his head so his black stetson blocked the sun. When he saw who had tapped him, Clifford said, "Oh, it is you Cross."

"Can you run her in for me?" Cross asked again. "The grey mare?"

Clifford nodded. "Yes Cross," he said. "It would be good to see if she still buck with a real cowboy in saddle."

Clifford shouted to his sons to hold the grey for another ride. Clifford's oldest boy George looked surprised until he saw Cross, then he called: "For Cross?"

When his father nodded, George looked pleased and said, "Oh-kay."

Although there were other fellows – like my brother Philmore – who tried, and did make the odd good ride, nobody in Snake Valley could match Cross for topping tough horses. They say that practice makes perfect and Cross got lots of practice. His regular riding horse was a wall-eyed cayuse named Skunk. Every morning when Cross stepped up into the saddle, Skunk would duck his head and buck like a black-and-white fiend for the first quarter mile. Cross always won the grunting, squealing, hoof-pounding tussle . . . but that never stopped Skunk from trying again the next morning.

Ferris shook my shoulder and said that another fellow had a horse in the chute and was getting ready to go. We tied our ponies in the shade and walked around to the west side of the arena and climbed up onto the fence. The planks were rough and grey and full of slivers so we settled our rear ends on them carefully. Our dog Caleb hunkered down with his nose over his paws to watch the show from under the bottom plank.

Nowadays rodeo arenas have whole banks of pipe steel, side-delivery chutes. But there was only one old-fashioned, straight-away wooden chute at Clifford's. When the front gate opened the bronc fired out into the arena head-first like a horse-flesh cannonball. Once a bronc came busting out of the chute, either the rider got tossed off or he rode his horse to a standstill – there was no eight or ten second time limit back then.

It was the younger of the Horvath twins, Norbert, who was getting ready in the chute. Norbert had his surcingle rigging cinched onto a snakey-looking bay. Orville, the other twin, stood beside and above the bronc, looking worried, like he was wanting to crawl down behind his brother and ride double. Norbert settled his rear end onto the horse's bare back; he jammed his right hand into the rigging's suitcase handle, lay back and swung his long legs up so that his boots rested over the bronc's shoulder. Norbert lifted his left hand, tried to grit his buck-teeth and nodded his head.

After the front gate flung open the bay fired straight out of the chute. It didn't slow down to buck or kick, it just raced hell-bent for election toward the far end of the arena. As the horse got closer to the plank fence you could tell Norbert was getting more and more nervous. His raised feet settled back towards the cinch and he started to lean farther forward. About ten feet from the fence, Norbert let go of the rigging and bailed off to the right. He hit the ground and spun-rolled up against the bottom plank. The bay cayuse's hooves scrabbled dust as it ducked its head to the left and ran down the fence away from Norbert. Orville jumped down from the chute and hurried down the arena to help his brother get up.

There were a few voices twittering on about how Norbert chickened out, but I for one sure couldn't blame him for bailing off.

I was sixteen years old and still hadn't climbed onto my first arena bronc. That was a tad embarrassing considering that Cross Harmon had started bronc riding at twelve and my older brother Philmore when he was thirteen. Our little brother Ferris had only just turned thirteen too, and he was chomping at the bit for a chance to show his stuff.

Philmore and Cross had stopped needling me about my reluctance to ride, but Ferris wouldn't let up. That spring he'd got to calling me "Pete," after Pete Knight, the world's champion bronc rider from Crossfield.

Me and Ferris were sitting side by side on the fence. We'd just finished arguing about who should milk the cows after the rodeo when Ferris elbowed me in the ribs and blurted out, "So, 'Pete,' you riding a bronc today? Or are you and me and the crows just straddling the fence again?"

Caleb must've understood the question. He swivelled his head and peered up at me with his curious-dog look. I just pretended I didn't hear the question. I ignored both Caleb and Ferris and glanced around the arena. It appeared that my reputation was still intact: even the Hutterite boys sitting close by didn't seem to have noticed what Ferris said. Like me, they enjoyed watching the Sunday rodeos but didn't ride themselves. They had a lot better excuse, though. Along with wearing the all black get-up that earned them Ferris's nickname of crows, not competing in rodeo events was part of their religion.

A lot of young ladies enjoyed watching the rodeo too, even the kerchiefed Hutterite girls. None of the women sat on the fence, though, they gathered in bunches and watched through the gaps between the planks. They weren't nearly as loud and noisy as us farm boys. They didn't yell, "Ride 'em cowboy!" or "Spur 'em!" or "Hook 'er Harry!"

If somebody got thrown off real hard the girls would all suck in a breath, then sigh it out as soon as the fellow got up. When somebody made a good ride they'd exchange smiling whispers and nod to one another. They never did get revved up like those hop-skip-and-jump football cheerleaders nowadays; but I suppose you'd expect more reserve from young ladies dressed in long blousy skirts and sun bonnets.

Two bunches of girls were gathered farther down the fence on the west side of the arena. Cross' and Philmore's girl Patsy Miller was there, and Dessie Nordmark. I waved at Dessie. Then I saw that Emeline Paladine, my girlfriend, was standing with the other bunch of girls and I waved at Emeline too.

When Cross and Philmore had sorted out the broncs they were going to ride, they nodded to Clifford Medicine Shield and sauntered down the fence past us, and stopped amongst the first bunch of girls. They had leaned against the plank fence and were visiting when Ferris hopped down and strutted towards them. I hopped down too, and Caleb and me followed.

Ferris stepped over to Philmore, puffed out his chest and said, "I want to ride today. Can you pick me out a bronc?" Ferris motioned back at me and added in an extra loud voice, "And pick a tough one Philmore, not some crow-hoppin' nag that brother 'Pete' here would be wantin' to try." The little devil turned towards me. He pushed out his chin, peered down his nose and snorted, "If 'Pete' ever got up the nerve to ride."

Those last words came out so loud I didn't have to look behind to know that even the Hutterite boys heard him. I'd taken a lot of guff from Ferris over the years, but his spouting off in front of everybody was just too much. I lifted my clenched fists and started for him.

Now my dog never did approve of us brothers fighting, so Caleb did what he thought was best. That darned mutt stepped between us, and I stumbled over him and landed fists and face first in the dirt.

When he saw what he'd done, Caleb sucked his tail between his legs and slunk over by the fence.

Ferris, he burst out laughing, and, when I looked up, I could see that most everybody was chuckling – Patsy and Philmore, even Dessie Nordmark had covered her mouth with her hand.

Cross Harmon wasn't laughing though. And from a distance, I could see that my girl Emeline was darned mad. I don't know whether it was because everyone else was laughing at "her" fellow, or because her fellow was dumb enough to put himself in a laughing-at position, but Emeline surely wasn't pleased.

My face was so red-hot it tingled as I stood up. I dusted myself off, took a deep breath and turned to Cross. I cleared my throat, sucked in some more air and said, "I'd sure appreciate it if you'd pick out a bronc for me, Cross. One a little tougher than what Philmore picks for Ferris."

After finishing my speech I wheeled away from the group and walked toward Clifford's barn. When Cross called me, I had to stop. I slowly turned around.

Ferris was still smirking and some of the other guys were holding back snickers, but not Cross. He asked if I wanted to borrow his surcingle. He said that considering this was my first time, I'd likely be more comfortable riding bareback rather than saddle bronc.

I was just about out of air but I managed to croak, "Sure thing. Thanks Cross," then I turned and started for Clifford's barn again. On the way past her, I nodded to Emeline.

After stepping through the door and out of general view, I stumbled down the alley and just plain collapsed onto a handy straw bale at the end of the barn. I was breathing fast and shallow. My insides ached like some big honker had punched me in the stomach.

My breathing was still coming fast when Caleb slipped through the door and padded down the alley to me. He set his sad-sack face in the dangerous spot between my shaking knees. I put out a trembling hand to stroke his head. Caleb's brown eyes looked about as guilty as they could be.

"Don't feel bad now Caleb," I said. "Maybe it's best I get this bronc riding business over with once and for all."

It wasn't as if I hadn't been bucked off before. I'd been tossed ass-over-tea-kettle plenty of times. Even our old saddle mare Dolly bucked me off once – after Ferris rammed a handfull of prickly speargrass under her saddle blanket. I have to admit that I was darned nervous about riding in front of a bunch of people, though. Besides, I couldn't help worrying about the kind of horse I might draw.

Clifford Medicine Shield claimed he could tell what kind of prospect a horse would be – just by the look in its eyes. If the horse was timid and wouldn't meet Clifford's gaze, then it'd most likely be a crow-hopper that'd only make a couple half-hearted jumps and quit. But if the horse glared right back at him, then Clifford figured it'd be a tough one – the kind Cross wanted – a rank bucker that would do its darnedest to toss the human monkey off his back.

Believe me or not, I hoped Cross would pick a rank one for me – something like the grey mare – a horse that would buck hard enough so that if I did get tossed off, I wouldn't feel too much the fool for it.

The type of horse that scared me was the kind Clifford Medicine Shield claimed you couldn't tell – until it showed its stripes in the arena: the crazy-scared kind that didn't buck at all, just ran, like the one Norbert had bailed off, like the one Cross drew at the first rodeo just the year before. That one was a bug-eyed sorrel gelding that Clifford figured should really buck. They pushed it into the chute and Cross strapped on his sur-cingle. After the gate opened, that sorrel renegade tore out of the chute and streaked across the arena. When it got to the fence it didn't turn like Norbert's, though, and Cross didn't bail off.

The sorrel smashed right through the bottom three planks. Cross's jaw busted the fourth, the top plank, and Cross was knocked out colder than a mackerel.

When we got him to town, it took Doc Headly a good half hour to wake Cross up, and fifteen stitches to sew the gash under his chin. A half-hour nap and a few more stitches didn't bother Cross any, though. What really upset him, was that that darned sorrel cayuse got away with his bareback rigging. He had to use Philmore's floppy old surcingle for the rest of the year and didn't get his own rigging back until six months later, after the horse roundup in the fall.

As I sat on that straw bale stroking my dog, I couldn't help remembering the sight and sound of Cross's chin whacking that plank.

There are some folks who enjoy committing brave and fearless acts out in public – and there are some of us that don't. That afternoon, though, I knew I couldn't back down, or everybody would figure I was the biggest chicken in all of Snake Valley.

Caleb gazed up at me with his wet brown eyes, and I was scratching his ears when Cross and Emeline walked into the barn. The two of them stood silhouetted in the door a second, waiting for their eyes to adjust to the dark. Then Emeline led the way over. She stopped in front of me. Emeline crossed her arms and wrinkled her brow in that way she has when she's mad.

"Cross tells me that you intend to ride a bareback bronc this afternoon," Emeline said. I looked up at her.

I was clearing my throat when she said, "You don't have to make a speech. Just tell me if you intend on riding today . . . yes, or no?"

I nodded.

Emeline shook her head. "Well if that isn't the dumbest thing I've heard," she said. Emeline turned away, then back towards me. "What do you intend on proving?" she said. "That your nose can shovel corral dirt as well as your brothers', and the rest of these so-called cowboys?" Emeline turned and touched Cross's shoulder. "Excluding you of course Cross."

I kept stroking Caleb but I didn't open my mouth. I was scared to death of what might come blurting out.

Emeline stamped her foot on the plank floor. "Well," she insisted. "Don't just sit there like a lump. Say something. Are you going through with this craziness?"

She stared at me so hard I had to lower my gaze and look down at Caleb. I could see the square light of the barn door reflecting in my dog's eyeballs.

"Everybody heard me," I muttered. "I gotta ride."

Emeline's voice lowered as she spoke my name. She leaned forward. When her fingers touched my shoulders, it felt like they tipped a hell of a big chip off.

"I know you're not afraid," she said, then more softly. "You don't have to prove anything to me."

Emeline isn't one to stay mushy-soft for long. "Not to anyone," she added firmly. She straightened up and carried on in her efficient, bustling voice. "Now," she said, "I've packed an afternoon snack big enough for the both of us – the three of us," she added, looking down at Caleb. "If Cross will get your horse, we can ride double down to the lake and eat lunch there."

As Cross turned and walked out, Emeline sat down on the bale, so close beside me her leg touched mine. She lay a hand on mine and stroked Caleb with her other one.

"Let's go to the lake," she said softly. "Please take us to the lake."

Emeline squeezed my hand and didn't say anything more.

It turned out little Ferris wasn't so smart after all. When his bronc tossed him into the fence he got a sprained wrist and a scrape and slivers across his forehead; our Mother wouldn't let him out of the house the next couple Sundays. Philmore got bucked off too, but Cross wowed the crowd with a wild-spurring performance on that hard-bucking, grey mare.

Caleb and me couldn't give you anything more than a second hand account of the proceedings, though. We missed the show that afternoon and had a nice quiet picnic down by the lake, with Emeline.

Harvest Breakup

After me and Emeline were married, I spent my happiest two months ever as we settled into our new life together. The wind blew hard every day and the sun shone down like a yellow-red demon, but that scorching weather meant there wasn't much summer-fallowing to be done. Caleb, he laid in the shade over by the barn and I concentrated my time on fixing up Fussy's old house, and on my new wife. It got so that, except for the blow-sand Emeline swept out the door every morning, we hardly noticed what was going on outside our own little lovenest.

Every good time comes to an end, though. Emeline had promised her parents she'd take the nurses' training she'd signed up for in the spring. The last week of August my dog and me drove her into Snake Valley to meet the Calgary train.

We stood out on the station platform and hugged and kissed and cried. Emeline promised she'd write me every Saturday, and I said I'd write her twice a week, and she said she would too then, so I said I'd write her every other day, and she smiled and said that sounded a great idea to her, so I said I'd write her a letter every day, after every meal, and it went on and on until the conductor come up to say the train was leaving, and stopped us before we promised to break ourselves on envelopes and paper and postage stamps.

Once she was inside her brick-red coach car, Emeline got up on her seat and slid the window down. She reached out a slim hand for me to hold. When that big train's brakes whooshed out a gust of steam and I had to let go, don't think Caleb and me didn't shed a few tears. And as the train clattered and rolled up the tracks, carrying our favorite girl to Calgary, my dog and me were both bawling like babies.

Maybe we had more reason to cry than we thought.

I hadn't noticed while Emeline was home, but my family hardly gave me the time of day. My Mother and my sisters and little brother Ferris were all still upset that me and Emeline had got married alongside Cross and Patsy Harmon. My older brother Philmore was more than upset. He was damned mad at me for standing up beside his former best friend and best girl. My Pa always tried to head off or stay out of family squabbles, but he never backed me on this, so I got to thinking that even he was siding with the others. Pa and Cross'd been close as a father and son, closer maybe – they were darned good friends – so I figured maybe he bore a grudge against me for Cross's marrying and moving out west. Pa probably missed Cross as much as Philmore missed Patsy.

All this unhappiness made for difficult times, especially during harvest.

That fall the wheat crops were sparse and they only stood about two feet high – so low, the binders could barely cut and tie the short stalks into bundles. Shaping those stubby bundles into proper pyramid-stooks was next thing to impossible, so Pa just let the piles lay where they dropped from the binder.

That saved some back-breaking work, but I for one wouldn't have minded keeping busier. At least during the day there were bundles to pitch, horses to drive and people sitting around the cook car at meal time – jawing at one another, if not at me. But after supper, when Caleb and me went back to our place, there was nothing to do, and nobody to visit – Cross was gone and the Horvath twins were busy with Dessie. I just didn't have any place to go.

Me and Emeline'd scrubbed and cleaned and painted Fussy's house, but you can't wipe away twenty years of living. Lying in bed at night, Caleb and me could smell Fussy and his cat Pearl.

Along with everything else, we couldn't afford to have Emeline bus home more than once every couple of months.

I felt so darned alone, you'd of thought I would have been writing to her every spare minute. And I did, for a while, but the letters were so depressing I couldn't hardly re-read them let alone mail them off to her. I'll tell you, my dog and me got awful tired of sitting around the house staring at one another.

As the good harvesting weather continued on up to the middle of September, the blisters on even the softest fellows' hands had hardened and turned to callouses, but the sore spots between me and my family didn't mend. Philmore especially seemed to get more and more obnoxious as time went on.

Since Fussy Warner died, Philmore had taken over operating the threshing machine and its engine. From his spot beside the engine he kept an eagle eye on me.

Now I'd never been known as one of the heavier loaders on our threshing crew, and with Philmore watching close, my loads got even lighter. I was so worried I'd miss my turn that I spent more time checking out the line at the separator than I did forking on a decent load. When I come driving in with my rack about half-empty, Philmore would look up and sneer at me. And as I waited in line, I'd just be dreading my turn at the thresher.

When the team pulled my bundle wagon alongside the machine, Philmore'd step up close and watch like a hawk as I forked those stubby bundles into the feeder. The little beggars were tough to handle, and if I fouled one up and it didn't all feed in head to butt Philmore chided and chafed at me. He'd never step up to help, but he'd sure watch and complain. I don't know anybody who can do a good job when they've all the time got a critic peering over their shoulder.

The only words my brother spoke to me that fall were: "Wise up will ya. You're pitchin' too slow," or "too fast," or, "You ain't settin' them on straight."

My little brother, Ferris, he'd turned fifteen in July and although our Mother and Pa had tried to talk him out of it, he didn't go back to school that fall. He was one happy camper for the first while. He was a tad small for pitching bundles yet, so he hauled grain to the elevator in town. The wind and the chaffy dust and the steady grind eventually got to him, though, and Ferris got to complaining about every little thing. One time he even blamed me because his hand-me-down boots didn't fit him proper! Ferris still got along with Caleb, though. After supper they wrestled and scrapped like they always did.

My mother only ever heard one side of the marriage story – Philmore's – so I don't suppose it's a surprise she sided with her eldest.

At meal times she didn't hold back food, but when she served me she just plopped my plate down heavy and turned away. If a fellow's pitching bundles, he can't hardly stuff enough inside to fill his stomach to last till the next meal, but Mother never offered me seconds. If I wanted more I had to walk up to the stove and ladle it out myself.

But the worst was when Philmore tied my poor dog up. Philmore claimed he was worried that "silly hound" might get tangled up in a belt or run over by a wagon. That was kind of odd, seeing as Caleb always stayed either under or on my bundle rack or plugged along behind it. And Fussy'd never had troubles with Caleb when he ran the threshing machine.

My poor dog just couldn't understand why Philmore tied him up; they'd been pretty good buddies in earlier times.

I was in line when Pa saw Caleb roped to the cook car, and he walked over and untied him. Philmore looked kind of sheepish and he whistled and slapped his thigh for Caleb to come, but my dog just turned sideways like he didn't see or hear anything. I figured that was pretty much fair – Philmore getting his own cold shoulder back.

Was I surprised when Philmore stood beside his open car door that night and called for Caleb to jump in with him.

"Come on Caleb," Philmore called. "Let's go for a drive."

My dog used to love to ride in Philmore's car, but this time he just turned the other way. Ferris, he laughed, and Philmore slammed the door shut. He spun gravel as he drove off. Pa watched the car drive away and shook his head. He nodded to Caleb and me before he left for home.

Well, it wasn't often Caleb turned down a ride in Philmore's car. I scratched him behind the ear and we headed back to our place.

That evening Pa had made a point of asking us to come over for the next morning's breakfast at the house. Normally we went over without an invitation, but that morning I decided to stay "home." Instead, Caleb and me fried up a pan full of bacon and eggs and sliced potatoes to go along with toast and coffee. I shared everything but the coffee with my dog – Caleb's never been much of a drinker.

Caleb's jilting Philmore didn't help my deteriorating relation-ship with my older brother. Philmore watched me twice as hard at the threshing machine. He got to watching and worrying me so close that he was ignoring his own job. One time the main drive belt loosened and spun off the tractor's drive wheel. Another time Philmore forgot to grease the fan gear and it heated and seized up – shut us down for a good half day.

It was almost funny when he blamed me for both problems. I had to keep from laughing when he claimed my rack swung in too close and knocked the drive belt off, and I did chuckle a bit when he said that my sloppy forking had got bundle chaff inside and gummed up the fan gear.

Whether anybody believed him or not I don't know, but nobody minded a break. We'd had a long stretch of good harvesting weather. But the little delays made Philmore even more ungodly irritable. He got so skittish it rubbed off on Pa and Ferris. They got to snapping at Caleb and me, and at one another. It didn't help that the crops were so poor a fellow often wonder-ed whether it was worth the trouble to thresh those miniature bundles.

A weather change near the end of September didn't help any either. Big soot-bottomed clouds rolled over the mountains and down to us from the northwest. Those black clouds smelled moist but there was no rain in them. They rumbled and threatened, even spit a few warning drops, then hovered over us until the wind changed and blew them away.

Those changing winds were hell on the harvesting crew. Clumps of prickly Russian thistles blew and rolled like tumbleweed across the field to pile up against one fenceline, then back to the other side when the wind changed. The jittery teams' ears flicked back and forth, and they spooked ahead when the dry, prickly things bounced past and around them.

At the threshing machine Philmore would start the day with the straw blower set to shoot its load east, then the wind would change and the dusty chaff would whirl and whip right into us and our horses' faces. Humans' and horses' (and even dog's) eyes would get to watering, and the scratchy chaff would slide down our shirts and prickle our sweaty backs. Eventually Philmore'd shut down and move the thresher – sometimes a couple times a day, but it seemed he'd only run the machine a half hour in a new spot before the wind would change again and be back blowing dust and chaff in our faces.

With the wind constantly whining, instead of just clucking our horses ahead to each new bundle pile, we teamsters got to barking at them. When we talked to one another we shouted too. Even the jokes that were told were mean and finished off with brittle-cackling laughs.

By the end of a windy day, our faces would be black as that fellow Al Jolson's – everything but the bloodshot pink of our eyes. Under our pants, our legs would be black up past the knees. Even with regular evening jaunts to the irrigation ditch, our bed-sheets quickly shaded from white to grey to black. Caleb he got so darned dirty, if he wagged his dusty tail too hard you had to dodge spurts of dirt.

Blow sand drifted around the window sills and the under door at Fussy's. Caleb and me were so sick of the wind by the time we got home, we just didn't feel like dusting and brooming the stuff out the door. I figured we'd have a clean-up day before Emeline came back for a visit the end of October. The dirt got so thick we could have planted peas or corn anywhere on the floor, and potatoes in the corners.

And I was so depressed and tired that after I finished reading or re-reading Emeline's latest letter I usually didn't have energy to write back to her but once a week at the best. Her letters started to tail off to only a couple times a week too.

Caleb and me, and everybody else I think, kept hoping that one time those dirty black clouds would drop a downpour of rain so's we'd have an excuse to stop but it didn't happen.

By the first of October, though, those clouds were smelling more and more like rain until one morning, when my dog and me stepped out of the house, it looked like a big cloud had touched down and covered the Buffalo Hills. By the time we finished feeding my mare Dolly and had breakfast ourselves, that thick grey bank of fog had flooded down and covered Snake Valley.

It's lucky we knew the way over to the homeplace by heart – in that thick, pea-soup fog I could barely make out the drops of moisture forming on the hair tips of Dolly's ears. Dolly just walked, and to make it easier to find the turn off into the yard, I rode the mare down along the right hand ditch. It seemed to take forever and about the time I figured we must have took the wrong trail I saw what looked like the homeplace's corner posts. Caleb, he made up my mind by sauntering through the gate. I clucked Dolly out of the ditch so's I could follow my dog up to the house before his wagging tail disappeared in the fog.

I had figured that we might not work that day. Pa, though, he wanted to get the last of the crop off. He said that the straw might be a little damp and tough, but he hoped the grain would still be dry enough to thresh. When I shrugged my shoulders, Philmore gave me a lecture on how folks should finish what they started. He went on so long that Pa had to tell him to stop and go out get his machines greased and fueled.

After I got my team harnessed and hitched to our rack I still couldn't see for fog, so Caleb lead the way and the horses followed him down to the south quarter. Once we were in the field I got off to load the rack. The damp stubble soaked my boots and pant-tops. It even flicked drops of dew up into my face as I bent down to fork and pitch stubby bundles over the high rack sides. The bundles were dripping with dew but after I crush-rolled a couple heads in my palm and chewed a handful of kernels, I found that they were bone dry and hard.

While I was forking on that first load, Philmore's big gas engine grumbled to a start. Hearing that engine noise was the only way I could tell where the threshing machine was once I'd loaded up. We just drove towards the engine noise.

Speaking of engine noise, I figured the machine didn't sound quite right that day – there was a kind of high-pitched squeal to it that a fellow heard better from a distance than up close. After I finished pitching off my second rack load, I got up enough nerve to mention it to Philmore. He snorted and asked what the blazes I knew about threshing machines. He said that I'd better start doing my own fair share of the work before I criticized him again.

It was a little cool that morning as well as damp. After I forked on my third load, Caleb and me huddled up close together on top of the bundle pile and I drove in behind Pa's big rack load on the lee side of the machine. The fog had lifted enough that I could easy make Pa out as he forked bundles off onto the chain feeder.

Pa must've noticed that whine in the machine too. Once he'd pulled out and I'd taken his place at the machine, Pa tied his lines to the front of his rack, jumped down and went over to discuss the matter with Philmore. Ferris, he'd just topped off a big wagon-load of wheat. He slipped down off his grain tank to join in with the conversation.

I couldn't see so well because of the fog, but both Ferris an Pa appeared to be pointing to one of the wind gears. That was where I figured the noise was coming from too.

Philmore is a stubborn sort. He shook his head and booted a cast iron tire, but eventually he signalled for me and the fellow on the other side to stop feeding the machine, then he stomped over to the big tractor and shut down the engine.

Caleb and me, we eased over to the machine to watch as Pa reached in and grabbed hold of that wind shaft and shook it. The darn thing wobbled and clanged. Philmore got out his hammer and pipe wrench and banged and wrenched at the gear.

Once it was off, Philmore looked up at me accusingly and said that gear'd been fine last night when he'd checked it.

He narrowed his eyes at me and said, "Since your sweet Emeline's gone, nobody knows what the hell you do at night."

I would've laughed at him, if I hadn't felt more like getting mad, or crying.

We had been going a long stretch without a break, and work-weary threshers had been known to toss a fork into the feeder to shut the machine down for a while, but heck, I never would've dreamed of doing such a thing myself.

Our Pa, he "tssk-tssked" Philmore, but he did give me a frown and a sidelong glance too. Caleb even looked me up and down once . . . and he'd been with me all the past night and morning. Talk about giving a fellow a case of the guilts.

Philmore figured Marchand's Emporium might have a new gear bearing. "If not," he said. "Then I'll have to drive all the way to Calgary to get the part." That's where he gave me an evil eye. "And you ain't invited to come along to see Emeline," he said. "If that's what you had in mind by loosening that gear pin."

Well I don't suppose a fellow could have looked more surprised than me at that comment – or guiltier, probably. My jaw dropped so's to leave my mouth gaping but I couldn't hardly say a word to defend myself.

Pa turned to look at me, and Ferris and Caleb too. Philmore, he grinned when he saw the effect he'd had. I don't suppose he believed what he'd said till then, but Philmore's eyebrows clumped together as he looked at me. He shoved the worn sprocket into my hand. "You get into Marchand's and see if they got this part," he ordered. "I'm gonna check over the rest of the machine. Just in case there's more loose pins."

Philmore turned to Ferris, "You'd best drive that load of grain into town too," he said. He flicked his thumb toward me. "And keep an eye on him."

When Ferris nodded, I just stood with that sprocket in my hand, staring at them both, dumb as a pole-axed bull.

Pa, he turned to me and said, "You'd better get going son. The sooner you get back the sooner we can get back to work."

Ferris said to Pa, "Why don't I just take the part along while I'm hauling the grain to town."

Pa started to nod, but Philmore frowned. "No way," he said. "Them that cause problems should fix them."

I was gettin' mad. "You take it in then," I said and held the gear out to Philmore. "You're supposed to be running this machine."

Pa, he thought a bit and said it would probably be better for me to take the part. I could ride one of my bundle horses into town and ride back quicker than Ferris.

Then Pa turned to Philmore and said he figured it would be a good idea to go over the machine with a fine tooth comb, considering the problems it had been having lately. "We're just about done for this year but it'd be nice to know the thresher's ready to go for next fall," Pa said. "Old Fussy used to check it over close before he shedded it in the fall."

Philmore nodded his agreement.

"And if you do find more worn-out parts," Pa continued looking at the gear I was holding (I guess he'd figured it couldn't have worn that bad after only a couple hour's work). "If you do find some more, then it would make a trip to Calgary worthwhile."

Caleb and me unharnessed my team. I tied Old King to my hay rack, then looped Sally's lines up so I could ride her. When I rode over to pick up the part, Pa said not to be in a big hurry, that it would take Philmore a while to finish checking out the machine. He handed me the gear and I slipped it over top of a hame. I squaw-reined Sally to the right and kicked her and we headed on a lumbering trot out of the field and onto the road. Caleb loped along ahead of us.

Ferris had already started out with the grain tank. After a quarter mile we trotted up beside his four-horse outfit. The morning sun shone out from under the lifting layer of fog and rimmed Ferris's heaped load of wheat with an amber glow.

When I rode alongside him I could see Ferris was really feeling his oats – his wheat actually. That load was heaped up so high, the wheat was touching the top of the tank all around the edges.

Ferris grinned at me and said, "I figure this one'll make the 'church load.'"

You see our parents always donated the heaviest load of the year to our church. Ferris wanted to be the driver to haul it in, so he heaped every load as full as could be. But it had been so dry for so long, that no matter how heavy he loaded, he hadn't been able to match the very first load that Pa had hauled in early September – back when the grain was a little tough and its plumpest and fullest.

As I rode Sally alongside the grain tank, Ferris kept reaching back and running his fingers through the grain and saying, "Feel this. Don't it feel a tad damp. She'll do it. Don't you think she'll make the church load."

When I reached down and scooped out a handful, a couple kernels tumbled over the side.

"Careful!" Ferris said sharply.

"It does feel a little damp," I said with a nod and Ferris smiled. But when I lifted my hand to pour the wheat into my mouth, he shouted angrily: "No. Don't. Put that back. You'll spoil my chances."

"I don't suppose one handful will make a difference," I said, but I did toss half the handful back on the load.

"Good," Ferris said. I chewed what I had left. "All of it." Ferris insisted. "Come on, spit it up."

I shook my head, "Nope. Don't want to spoil your sample with my spit," I said. I touched Sally with my heels and she lumbered off. "See you in town," I shouted over my shoulder.

Ferris cursed after me as I rode off under the lifting lining of fog.

Both me and the worn sprocket bounced and bumped along as Sally lumber-trotted down the road. By the time we got to town, the sun had burnt off all but a few whisps of fog. I tied Sally up outside Marchand's Emporium and swallowed the gummy wad of wheat before I went inside.

When I plunked the sprocket onto his counter, Mr. Marchand frowned. He lifted it up by the worn teeth and turned the sprocket around to find the part number. He pursed his lips and shook his head.

"I do not believe I have one of these," he said. "But it will only take a few moments for me to look. Do you have the time?"

Now, whenever Mr. Marchand said, "Do you have the time?" you knew you were in for at least a half hour's wait. I don't know what he did in the back, but it wasn't often he found what he was looking for. There wasn't much I could do, though.

"Sure," I said. "I got time." Mr. Marchand nodded, but he almost forgot to take the sprocket with him as he stepped into the back storage room.

I'd written a long note to Emeline over the last couple nights, so I called to Mr. Marchand to say that I would be over at the post office if he wanted me. Caleb and me stepped out of the store and across the street.

We walked up onto the wooden sidewalk and into the post office. I passed two pennies over the counter to Mrs. Johansen and she gave me a stamp. As I licked and pasted it on Emeline's letter, Mrs. Johansen fingered through one of her postal slots.

"O-ho. Here it iss," she said happily. "I vas priddy shur you hat another letter from yur priddy little missus." She handed me an envelope: it was powder blue, part of some stationery I'd given Emeline for her birthday.

Mrs. Johansen set her heavy elbows on the counter and leaned over as I slit the letter open with my jack-knife. She's a fine woman, but I wasn't going to read the letter in front of her. I smiled, said, "Thank you, Mrs. Johansen," and stepped out the door.

"You're velcome," she called after me.

I sat on the bench next to mainstreet's water trough, slipped out and unfolded the letter. It was three pages long.

Caleb sat down directly in front of me and perked his ears up to hear what Em had to say. I checked around. The local wags were all in their chairs, propped against the pool hall wall and dozing. They were a good half block south and across the street. I figured it was safe to read the letter out loud.

'My dearest husband, [and Caleb]' (Em didn't write that but I added it for my dog's sake).

'I do hope you are [both] happy and healthy and that the family is treating you [both] better.'

"Well," I said, grinning at Caleb. "Two out of three ain't bad."

Caleb whimpered impatiently so I carried on: *'The nursing courses are not particularly difficult, but we do work quite long shifts. I understand this is meant to weed out the uncommitted. You should know that their attempts have no chance of uprooting me. I am as deep-rooted and tenacious as a Canada thistle. I don't know whether I am capable of becoming a competent nurse . . . '*

"Why of course you are Emeline. Nobody would make a better nurse," I said to the letter. "Right Caleb?" My dog licked my hand.

'But you know that I shall give my best possible effort. It seems so long ago that we last spoke, and yet it was little more than a month — four weeks and six days to be exact. I miss you [both]. I miss your gentle touch. My lips . . . ' I checked across the street. It looked to me like one of the wags had eased forward and perked a cauliflower ear towards us. I checked over my right shoulder . . . I was sure I saw Mrs. Johansen's head duck back from the post office window. I skimmed quick over the next page and a half of the letter.

"We'll just save this part for tonight," I told Caleb. Then started in a spot I figured would be safe.

'The head nurse, Mrs. Cockwell, has been very helpful. She seems to have taken a particular interest in me. I have told her of our decision and she has offered to advise me in the safest, most effective birth control pract . . . '

"Oops," I said. "Better go on a little further."

As I skimmed over Em's large flowing script a train whistle blew as a diesel engine puffed up the tracks toward town. I turned on the bench and Caleb and me watched it slow and stop just past the elevators. The conductor hopped down and levered a switch. The engine's wheels spun a little then caught and the whole train started to back onto the open sidetrack in front of the big-shouldered, white Alberta Grain elevator.

I turned and looked across the street. A couple of the local wags had shifted forward on their chairs and sat with elbows on their knees peering at the train. Both old fellows had striped engineer's caps perched on their heads, so I figured they'd be watching close to see whether the young railroad turks fouled up their old jobs.

I watched them until something farther to the left caught my eye. It was Ferris's outfit prancing toward town with the big load of grain. When they got closer, his four horse team and big load looked pretty impressive – especially when they rolled down the town's main street.

Ferris had a couple colts hooked on wheel, Pincher and Baldy, a pair of youngsters that Cross Harmon had started driving that spring; and they obviously hadn't heard a train huffing and puffing and banging rail cars around before.

The young wheelers held their heads high and their eyes were open wide and their ears perked forward. Even the old lead team had their heads up and were watching as their hairy legs pranced them down main street. With that big load of grain to pull, little Ferris was able to keep a grip on the lines, brace his feet and keep them down to a fast walk. The cocky little character didn't look even a tad worried, though. Except that he kept checking over his shoulder to make sure the horses' speedy gait wasn't jiggling any wheat off his potential church load.

The farm wags that hadn't budged when the train whistle sounded, they perked up at the rattle of trace chains and rumble of wagon wheels. A couple of the old fellows pointed to Ferris. I don't know whether they were impressed with the load, or the young excited wheelers – maybe both.

As Ferris got close to them, one old geezer – it was old "Uncle Billy" Fowler – he eased out of his chair and limped down off the wood sidewalk. Uncle Billy raised a bony hand to Ferris and the kid "whoa-ed" the team. The old fellow kneed his way up onto the front wheel, reached over the side of the tank and scooped a handful of grain. Right after Uncle Billy slid down off the wheel, the train-brakes let out a whooshing hiss and Pincher and Baldy jumped forward.

Ferris just nodded at Uncle Billy, and drove on like he had meant to leave then. The oldtimer shuffled back up onto the sidewalk and dribbled a portion of wheat into the cupped hands of his fellow wags. They all looked back at the load and nodded their heads. The wags knew about Pa's big September load, and the way they were nodding, it looked like they figured Ferris was hauling a heavier one.

Caleb and me watched as Ferris headed up the ramp and into the elevator. Jock Primrose must have figured the young wheelers might cause trouble because he slid the elevator doors shut, both front and back.

After the doors closed, I went back to reading Emeline's letter. I didn't get much read though, because the train had really got to banging and slamming behind us. I figured it was lucky Jock shut the doors because Pincher and Baldy would be really fidgeting while the grain tank got lifted and emptied behind them.

Ferris was in the elevator so long I guessed Jock must've been figuring out whether that one was the church load, and when Ferris came driving out of the elevator I knew it must have been the big one, because the kid was grinning from ear lobe to ear lobe. He lifted one arm and waved the weigh ticket to me. I didn't hear what he yelled because right then the train's brakes really hissed and two empty cars smacked together and boomed like big, hollow metal drums.

Pincher and Baldy had had enough of noises. They jumped ahead so hard they smacked the double trees into the lead team's rumps, and the whole outfit was off and running!

Cocky little Ferris still had all four lines in one hand. When the horses jumped ahead, they jerked that hand ahead and spun Ferris around. He barely stopped himself from tumbling over the front of the wagon, but he did drop his right lead line. He reached over to try to grab it again, but the leather line slithered over the front of the box, down onto the pole and from there onto the dirt. While Ferris was hunting the loose line his spooked horses were gaining speed. Even the old leaders, Wally and Jack, had perked up. They looked game for a good blow-out run.

Caleb, he jumped down off the boardwalk and ran alongside the wagon, barking, but that just spooked the young wheelers worse. Ferris was leaning over the front of the wagon trying to decide how to snare the lost line when it got tangled up in the right front wheel and began wrapping around the wheel hub. When that line started tightening, the old lead team responded by lumbering to the right. Little Ferris hauled back on the brake lever and pulled hard on the remaining three lines, but it was too late.

The lead team's noses cramped right and they swerved straight toward the pool hall. As the horses and the empty grain tank clattered and rattled towards them, the local wags' eyes widened. They deserted their chairs and scattered like spooked partridge, scurrying up both sides of the sidewalk – all the time looking back over their shoulders, waving their arms and squawking, "Whoa! Whoa now! Whoa!"

Finally, the double-taut lead line snapped and the leaders' heads were free . . . just as they jumped up onto the sidewalk. Boards crashed and splintered under-hoof as Wally and Jack clambered on up until their heads draped over the top of the pool hall's split door.

Standing right behind the leaders, with their front feet up on the sidewalk too, and trembling with the excitement of the race, were Pincher and Baldy. And right behind them sat Ferris, up on the wagon seat, still clutching three lines in one hand and the weigh ticket in his other.

Caleb gave one, last, useless bark as Uncle Billy Fowler shuffled back down the sidewalk. When he was about level with

Ferris and the wagon seat, Uncle Billy plucked the scrunched weigh ticket from Ferris's hand.

He smoothed it out and looked at it, then lifted it up. "Yep," he called over his shoulder to the farm wags. "Looks like the kid hauled in the church load."

Uncle Billy turned and handed the slip back to Ferris, and as he did, he spoke real loud for his half-deaf audience: "But you know young fellow, you sure didn't have to go to all this trouble just to show us the ticket."

Well, Uncle Billy chuckled like a crazy cricket at his own joke and the rest of the wags, their old tickers hadn't beat so fast for decades and they were hepped up, well, the laughs just burbled and hiccupped and farted out of their puckered up mouths.

Now, if there's something that Ferris detests more than anything in the world, it's being laughed at. He could've laughed along with them wags, but he didn't. He turned away from those fellows. First he glowered down at Caleb, then across the street at me.

Ferris didn't say a word all the time the wags and me helped untangle the line from his wheel and rivet it back together, and then back his outfit off the sidewalk. Once everything was in place, he climbed back up on the seat, snatched the lines from my hand, and drove off down the street – without a word of thanks to any of us. And he was still leaving quite a repair job behind. Since it was my brother and our outfit that wrecked the sidewalk, I figured it behooved me to help repair it.

Mr. Marchand came over with some two-by-ten planks and it took us a half hour to replace the broken boards. After we finished, Mr. Marchand told me he hadn't been able to find that sprocket for the threshing machine.

By the time Caleb and me got home, the story of Ferris's wreck had changed considerably from what I remembered. There was no mention of the train, little brother blamed the runaway on Caleb's barking and spooking his team into the pool hall. He also said he'd caught me reading Emeline's letter instead of riding back to say there weren't any sprockets at Marchand's. But that was a pretty minor offence compared to: "Caleb's almost killing our youngest child . . . again," as our Mother put it. She was referring to an incident that occurred at the Snake Valley race-meet a couple years before.

I was already deep in the dog house and now Caleb was crammed right in beside me. It didn't do me any good to explain what really happened, or to suggest they ask Uncle Billy Fowler, because nobody would listen.

Since Marchand's didn't have the part, there was no more work to be done that day, so Caleb and me rode back to Fussy's old place. I wasn't surprised that Philmore didn't offer to take Caleb and me to Calgary with him.

Like any other human body, I've made my share of mistakes, and I don't mind taking the blame for them, but I sure didn't appreciate my dog and me getting blamed for something we didn't do.

After I'd settled down enough, I sat down to finish reading Caleb the rest of Emeline's letter. I'd got to the last page:

'As I said earlier my darling[s]. I hope that you and your family are sorting out your difficulties. If not, please know that I love you. I miss you [both] so much. Please write soon.

XXXXOOOOXXXXXOOOOO

With my deepest love,

Your Emeline.'

You just don't know how much that letter meant to me. I read the last part over a couple more times, even let Caleb sniff the last page. Emeline had sprayed a wisp of her cologne on it. Caleb likes the smell of lavender.

That night Pa rode over to say that Philmore had fixed the threshing machine but that he figured that they could finish the field themselves in the morning. Pa looked down at me and said, "You must have some fixing up to do around this place to keep you busy, don't you son?"

After I agreed that there was always something that needed fixing, he nodded to me and Caleb, and reined his horse away. God that man sat a horse well: ramrod straight, whether he was walking, trotting or loping, just like he was a part of the animal. I can still remember standing at the door that evening and watching his broad-shouldered back get smaller as he travelled down the road away from us.

By the middle of the next afternoon, Caleb and me were over cleaning out the barn when a bank of towering black rain clouds formed over the mountains, and a gusting wind come blowing in from the northwest.

I guess everyone was in a hurry trying to finish the field before the storm hit, and Philmore and Pa had an argument about whether to move the threshing machine because of the wind change. When Pa went to move it himself, he didn't fold the chain feeder up before he backed the tractor into the thresher. When he went to stop, the hand clutch-lever didn't catch, so the tractor kept backing and the feeder drove into Pa's back; it crushed him against the steering wheel before the tractor finally stopped.

Philmore drove like a fiend to get Pa to the Cluny hospital, and he got him there alive, but Pa was hurt so bad he died the next morning.

I always felt it was partly my fault. If I'd been there and they'd had one more hand around, they might've been done before the storm hit.

I guess that's what the rest of the family must've thought too. At the funeral Caleb and me and Emeline all stood off to one side – with Cross and Patsy Harmon. None of my family said a word to any of us.

Emeline and I had talked things over the night before. When the funeral was over, we all went back to Fussy's, and Cross helped me load our stuff into his truck. He was going to haul it out west to Ridgeview for us.

Cross had said that he knew a fellow there needed help gathering and wintering his cows. That meant Caleb and me would spend the winter in a range cabin moving cows from haystack to haystack, but that was fine because Emeline had to go back up to Calgary to the hospital anyway.

Before we left for Ridgeview, Emeline tried to get me to stop by and at least say goodbye to my mother and sisters, but I just couldn't go, I felt too damned hurt.

My Outriding Career

"That was sad Grandpa," sniffed Katie.

"Yes," Patti agreed, "really sad."

"It sure was," I sighed, as I reached up to rub a speck of dirt outa my right eye. I looked down at those long-faced girls and eased my hand down to stroke my chin.

"So I guess I'll just have to tell you an exciting story now," I piped up, "about horses, and chuckwagon racing, and Caleb and me."

The girls, they brightened up some, and leaned forward as I started telling them about my outriding career.

Was I ever excited when Gimp MacLean asked me to outride for him at the 1935 edition of the Calgary Stampede chuckwagon races. Sure, old Gimp did wallow near the bottom of the chuck-wagon barrel, but a shiny-assed rookie like me couldn't expect to start at the top.

I considered it quite a feat to get picked as an outrider. When I told my wife Emeline, though, she wasn't impressed . . . or pleased.

Emeline likes watching rodeos and horse races but she never has been keen on watching me compete. She says I'm too darn clumsy and absent-minded. And she especially didn't like the idea of my riding behind a chuckwagon after the older nurses told her that a steady stream of those crazy "wagonmen" got packed into the hospital every July.

Emeline has never forgot or forgave me for outriding that summer. She'll tell you even now: "I warned the bloody fool not to do it, but do you think he ever listens to me!"

Gimp MacLean's son Rusty and my best friend Cross Harmon were more helpful. They'd both rode before and the first morning of the show they gave me all kinds of outriding tips: don't let your horse have too much line; grab your tent peg low down; don't use your stirrup to mount; jump your horse after you're past the top barrel; don't bump the other outriders; look both ways before you ride onto the track; keep your eyes and ears open; and darned sure don't ever be late.

After those two had finished, so many do's and don't's were buzzing in my head, I could barely remember my name.

Rusty MacLean could tell I was a little muddled I guess and needed a chance to clear my head. After lunch, he led Caleb and me across the Elbow River and we all three climbed to the top of Scotchman's Hill. Rusty plunked down with his long legs dangling over the edge of the hundred foot high bank, but me, I settled into an Indian squat a good six feet from the crumbly edge. Caleb flopped down next to me and set his muzzle on my lap.

From up there we had a grand view of the half-mile oval racetrack that Gimp's chuckwagon and our outriding horses would be circling that night. Rusty pointed to where the track gapped into a half-moon infield, right in front of the big flat-roofed grandstand. He said that infield gap was where the chuckwagons made their figure eight turns around the barrels before charging onto the racetrack.

The Stampede grounds pretty much filled a three cornered space between a bend in the river and downtown Calgary. Scattered along the grounds between the track and the log gates of old Fort Calgary were stock barns, the Gayland Shows mid-way and a teepee-topped Indian Village. The aroma of candy apples, buttered popcorn and mustard-slathered hotdogs drifted up to us. Even from up on the hill we could hear cane-twirling carnies calling the nearest sucker, squeals and screeches from the roller coaster ride, and heavy, slow drumbeats and chants from moccasin-shuffling Blackfoot and Stoney Indian dancers.

With the people speckling the grounds like confetti and the teepees and the red and white tents and the tall, glittery ferris wheel it was sure colorful but, being prairie born and raised, both my dog's and my eyes couldn't help sliding back to gaze at the awe-inspiring Rocky Mountains. Even though they peaked fifty miles to the west of us, that afternoon those blue-grey giants appeared to loom right over downtown Calgary's shoulder and peer down at the grounds too.

As my gaze finally dropped from the mountains a big boxy building, squatting about a half mile away, caught my eye. I pointed it out to Rusty.

"Why that's the Holy Cross Hospital," said Rusty. "You should know that – Emeline is training there."

"No wonder it seemed familiar," I said. I stroked Caleb behind the ears. "It's too bad Emeline's working during the day. I bet she'd love to see the view from up here."

Rusty smiled and said, "The best time to take your lady to Scotchman's Hill is at night – for the fireworks display after the races. Believe me," he added with a wink. "Those colored explosions look ten times brighter with a pretty gal's head resting on your shoulder."

We sat and soaked up the sun for half an hour before traipsing back down the hill and across the river. Rusty carried on over to the infield to watch Cross Harmon rope, but Caleb and me stayed at the barn and had a nap. We wanted to be rested up so we could take Emeline to Scotchman's Hill after the races.

By seven o'clock that evening, me and Rusty and Cross were all riding our horses behind Gimp's chuckwagon. It rolled along like a green and yellow prairie schooner in the middle of a long line of wagons and outriders that snaked from the barns over to the race track. White-hatted, western-shirted spectators were packed like standing-sardines six deep on either side of the road.

They pointed and waved as each wagon's iron-rimmed wheels rumbled past.

My horse danced a prancy, clackity-clack side step down the pavement. He was a half-thoroughbred stud named Bully Sir. I wasn't real pleased to be riding a stud, but I'd told Gimp that I could handle anything, and a fellow has to measure up to his bragging level, I guess. Besides, Bully was supposed to be blazing fast.

Emeline had run over to the wagon barns after classes at the Holy. She'd made it just in time to crawl into the back of Gimp's wagon, and was kneeling and checking out the scenery from behind the end gate.

With me sitting tall on my prancing mount and duded up in Gimp's fancy green and yellow satin shirt, I thought she might have felt a tad proud of me – might even have gotten over being mad at me for outriding. We couldn't talk because of the clatter and rattle of the wagon, but Emeline did appear to be in good spirits. She was smiling as she swivelled her head from side to side to take everything in.

Caleb crouched down below her – in the bottom of the wood and canvas basket Gimp used to hold his stove. Caleb's eyes were big and round and shiny, with the whites showing around them. He peered over the edge of the rack at the big crowd and clipped the ends of his toenails with his teeth.

He could have been a bit worried about Rusty's dog-hating mare too. But I figure Blaze was too busy to notice Caleb. Rusty kept pirouetting her around and around so he could wave his stetson to impress the young ladies in the crowd. That red-headed devil even made eyes at my woman a couple times.

There were four fellows dressed in white aprons and cowboy hats standing on either side of the backfield gate. They were taking tickets. I tipped my head so they could see the "Contestant" badge pinned to the front of my new stetson. Emeline didn't have a pass; she ducked down where they couldn't see her.

Since Gimp didn't race until the fourth heat, he parked his outfit with the leaders standing head-first against the infield corrals. Rusty and Cross were outriding in the first couple races. They tied Gimp's outriding horses to the plank fence close to the wagon, then ran off to find their mounts for the first heat. I sure wanted to watch those races but I knew I didn't dare tie Bully Sir up. It took a considerable amount of sweet-talking, but I finally persuaded Emeline to hold the stud for me, and Caleb and me ran down the alleyway and into the infield.

We made it just in time to see the first outfits roll into position beside their track-side barrels. Caleb assumed a point position when he sighted Cross and Rusty. I knew I'd be stationed in behind Gimp's wagon, throwing a tent peg, so I ignored the fellow up front grabbing hold of the lead team. I studied the other fellows that led their horses in behind the wagon to set up a make-believe chuckwagon camp. Rusty and the other peg man reached into the back of their wagon and each pulled out a five foot long tent peg. The tops of the pegs were attached to a canvas flap that stretched out over the stove rack when they set the pegs on the ground. The fellows had their pegs set wide enough that Cross could hunch under that canvas flap, grasping either corner of a cast iron stove – he had his horse's lead line clamped in his teeth.

When the starting klaxon sounded, Cross heaved the stove into its basket rack. Rusty and his partner chucked their tent pegs into the back of the wagon, then they all led their horses after the lumbering rig. As the wagon circled right around the top barrel, Rusty grabbed his saddle horn and swung up into the saddle – without touching a stirrup. I couldn't see them in behind the turning wagon but Cross and the other two riders must've mounted just as quick, because all four of them followed the wagon's swerving tracks around the bottom barrel and onto the track.

The four wagons' white tarps flapped and rippled as they raced side by side into the first turn, just ahead of a trailing swarm of outriders.

Because the infield corrals blocked my view, I climbed up onto a bronc chute to watch the rigs race around the second turn.

Down the backstretch, the inside chuckwagon started to pull away, leaving the other three wagons running in a rising cloud of dust. The swarm of outriders had moved to the outside of the track. The riders crouched behind their horses' flowing manes, their stetson hat brims flattened back to match their horses' speed-flattened ears.

After rounding the third and fourth turns, the leading wagon began to lose ground. The worried driver looked over his shoulder then collected all four lines in one hand, grabbed his whip and snap-cracked it above the backs his tiring team. Caleb stopped whining to turn and watch the wide nostriled horses race down the homestretch towards us. The thud of hooves and rattling of trace chains mixed with loud, "Geeyah . . . Geeyaah's!" from line-slapping drivers, and warnings of, "Coming through!" or, "Get the hell out of my way!" from the outriders.

The grandstand crowd stood and roared as two faster-finishing outfits gained ground on the leading wagon. The horses and wagons thundered across the finish line in a three way dead heat for first.

Whew. That was the first chuckwagon race I'd seen and it had my heart just a'thumping.

I lifted Caleb onto the chute so he could watch the backstretch run of the second race. We stayed for the start of the third heat, too, but before those wagons crossed the finish line, my dog and me ran back down the alley to fetch my horse.

When we got back, Emeline's happy smile had disappeared. She jammed Bully's lead rein in my hand and cussed me out for having left her to mind a spoilt horse that had only one thing on his mind.

"You two deserve one another," she said and stamped away. Caleb he gave me a look, then trailed after Em with his head drooping and his tail sucked between his legs.

I soon found out what had upset her. A fellow named Quincy Billingsgate had parked his outfit next to Gimp, and Quincy's left-hand leader, a chestnut mare, was in season. Right after I got back, the mare flipped her tail in the air and sidled towards the stud. Bully was interested in meeting her too. He arched his neck and pawed the dirt, then he whinnied and tried to pull away. He tugged so hard I marvelled that Em's skinny arms had been able to hold him.

Rusty showed up as Gimp MacLean eased his outfit away from the corrals. Rusty said we'd best follow his dad's wagon into the infield. I swung into the saddle and, with a couple taps from my quirt, convinced Bully to leave his new-found lady love.

As we rode down the alleyway towards the half-moon infield a dull, tight ache filled the space behind my breast bone, and my knees felt so trembly and weak I could barely hold my feet in the stirrups. I couldn't help wondering whether those ancient Romans felt something the same when they drove their chariots into the forum for their first – and maybe their last – performance.

Caleb and Emeline were standing next to the infield gate. I nodded to them as we pranced past – my dog looked worried, my wife still looked mad. Rusty, he chirped something I didn't catch, but whatever he said made Emeline's tight lips curve into a grudging smile.

Me and Rusty followed Gimp's chuckwagon around the bottom of number three barrel and out onto the track. Instead of following the wagon down the track to the first turn we reined our horses to the right and stepped off in front of the grandstand stage.

Rusty stepped over close to the stage and motioned me to follow. "Come over here," he said. "I've got something important to show you."

I led Bully over and watched as Rusty jammed his right boot heel deep into the track dirt.

"There's soft spots like this all along the stage," Rusty said. "It's where they dig the posts in for an extra platform they set up after the races – for the grandstand show and the fireworks." Rusty squinched the heel of his boot deeper into the soft dirt close to the stage. "So don't go running that stud too close to the outside, or he'll trip in one of them soft spots," Rusty warned.

After I nodded, Rusty stepped back and hopped bum first onto the grandstand stage.

I tried hopping up too, but my weak knees gave out on me. I elbowed my way beside Rusty, then glanced over to where Emeline was kneeling in front of the chutes, with her arms wrapped around Caleb's neck. When my dog saw me looking at him, he flip-flopped his tail in the dirt. Emeline smiled and lifted her arm. Both me and Rusty waved back at her.

Gimp MacLean's had been the first outfit to enter the infield so me and Rusty got to watch the rest of the rigs file down the alley into the infield. I winced when I saw Quincy Billingsgate's lead team coming our way. The stud noticed too, but he wasn't displeased. He tugged on the lead line and whinnied at that chestnut mare.

The mare whinnied back as Quincy tried to steer his outfit around the bottom of number four barrel and onto the track. That ornery mare pushed and egged her right-hand lead partner towards us until he shoulder blocked the bottom barrel of number three. First the wheelers, then the wagon's axles clanged and clunked over the steel barrel. It tipped over and jammed between the hind axle and Quincy's low-slung, iron stoverack where it scraped and squealed – metal against metal – until Quincy stopped his outfit to let the track crew pry it out.

When Cross Harmon loped his horse over to join us, Bully was whinnying and craning his neck towards Quincy's mare. Cross said that me and him could sure trade horses, but the wall-eyed, hammer-headed cayuse Cross was riding didn't look like much of a prize either.

I said: "No thanks Cross, I'll ride what I got."

The three of us stood together visiting and watching the wagons make their practice barrel turns. I wasn't so nervous until the four rigs swung around and lined back towards the infield to prepare for the race. Then my heart started pounding double time. It seemed to take forever, but eventually the wagons on barrels' one and two rolled up the track past us. Gimp nodded to us as he drove in and Cross and Rusty hurried in behind the wagon. I shuffle-stepped after them.

Right away Bully saw Quincy's mare over on barrel four. He whinnied. The mare answered, and ducked and swung her rear end under her tug and towards us. Bully tried to trample over top of Cross as he set the tin stove behind Gimp's stove-rack. I was so busy keeping the stud away from Cross that I barely got my tent peg pulled out and set on the ground before the klaxon sounded.

I heaved the peg back into the wagon box and led Bully up alongside the moving wagon. Gimp's outfit was circling the top barrel when Rusty shouted for me to, "Jump!"

I grabbed my saddle horn. But as I started to swing on, Bully shied away from me and left me dangling half-on, half-off the saddle. I was trying to scramble the rest of the way aboard, when Quincy's lead team sidled over into our area and smacked me in the back. The collision knocked me to the ground and I curled into a knee-cuddling position just as Quincy's lead team, then his wheelers clumped by on either side of me. Next Quincy's wagon box blocked out the sun as it eased over top of me. The wagon came to a stop with its barrel-bashing stove rack an arm's length from my head.

I had just rolled onto my hands and knees when Caleb scuttled under the wagon and grabbed my shirt cuff. With his hind feet scratching dirt, my dog jerked my sleeve and dragged me out between the wagon's front and hind wheels.

When I stood up, I heard Quincy Billingsgate cussing a blue streak at somebody or something. Caleb tried to drag me towards Emeline and the chutes, but I stopped to see who or what Quincy was yelling at. The object of his displeasure turned out to be my former mount. Bully was standing beside Quincy's lead mare making a pitch for her favors.

I figured that was a real break for me. My outriding horse was still available!

But Caleb didn't want me to go. Our quick tug of war ended with a "rrrip" and him ending up tail first in the dirt with my yellow shirt cuff in his mouth.

Cuffless but free, I ran over and grabbed Bully's lead line. I got to him just before he chinned his way up onto the hunkered down mare. Some of the raunchier spectators groaned in disappointment as I jumped into the saddle and tapped Bully with my quirt to egg him out onto the track.

The stud stumbled along for a ways, swinging his head from side to side, trying to turn back. But after a couple more quirt swats Bully's racing instincts overcame his passionate ones, and he started to stretch out and run. He cruised around the first two turns hugging the inside so close that my left stirrup scraped white paint off the rail.

Down the backstretch the evening sun glared through the billowing dust and I couldn't see so I squinted my eyes shut. When I opened them around the last turn Bully was really motoring and we were closing fast on the trailing outfits. I let the stud angle to the outside to go around them. When we drifted out of the dust, I could see that Gimp's green and yellow wagon was dropping back. His horses were running out of steam.

I smiled because I knew Bully could catch him. I wouldn't be late on my first ride.

As we raced down the homestretch I noticed Quincy Billingsgate's outfit still parked in the infield. Bully saw Quincy's tail-switching mare and tried to angle towards her. I had to really pull on my right rein to keep him running along the outside of the track.

When Rusty yelled: "Get away from there," I remembered his warning about the soft spots along the stage. But it was too late. Bully stumbled. His front end dropped from under me and I sailed head first onto the track.

I came to slowly – in a bed – in a strange smelling, eye-blinking bright room. A lady dressed in white and grey was bending over me. For a second or two I figured I'd made it to heaven. I knew I was mistaken when the nurse jabbed a needle into my behind.

A few minutes later Rusty and Emeline sauntered into the room. My wife eased out from under Rusty's arm, ran over, and turned a couple cracked ribs into broken ones with a sobbing big hug. After the pain in my ribs subsided, I noticed that my right shoulder hurt.

"Dr. Simpson says you broke your collarbone," Emeline explained. "You were lucky not to be hurt a lot worse. That stallion rolled right over top of you."

"Don't worry about Bully, though," Rusty added with a smile. "He wasn't hardly shook up. After doing a head-over-tail somersault, he jumped up and loped across the track to renew acquaintances with Quincy's mare."

Emeline's cheeks colored as Rusty declared: "Those two horses' antics were the hit of the night's show. More of a sensation even than your own clowning and acrobatics."

We had only talked a few minutes when the nurse reappeared and told us that it was way past visiting hours. Rusty, he left then but Emeline took a step closer.

"We have to go anyway," she said as the nurse took her arm. "Rusty promised that we could watch the fireworks together." The nurse was hustling her out the door when Emeline called over her shoulder, "From up on Scotchman's Hill."

Less than an hour later the fireworks started. From where I sat the sounds of the explosions were just soft "poof-poofs," but I could see the whole light show framed in my east-facing window. It was quite a sight with those pretty colors streaking up, splishing and splashing against the night sky, then trickling back to earth.

I really enjoyed the performance, but I couldn't help glancing past the flashes to Scotchman's Hill. I sure hoped that Emeline and Rusty had taken Caleb with them.

What with the day's excitement, and the exploding colors and noise, I knew my poor dog would have got awful upset if they left him down at the barn all by himself.

Waiting For Gold

There's something about a hefty nugget of gold that makes for a fonder feeling than you can get from a whole wheelbarrow full of paper money. The paper you want to wheel down to the bank and shove across a teller's counter – but not the gold. That hefty nugget feels so good resting in the palm of your hand . . . your thumb can't help but stroke down into the glimmering hollows and over the smooth edges. And once it's snuggled safe in your grip, that nugget feels so comfy-warm you never want to give it up. No, not ever!

I don't doubt that it was that same feeling attracted thousands of prospectors to the ice-cold gravel of the Klondike and the Cariboo, and the same sensation that warmed the cockles of the young ladies who followed them there to share in the grubby fellows' pain and pleasure.

Caleb and me – we weren't immune – we caught a bout of gold fever once ourselves. But the closest we came to discovering a motherlode was watching the morning sun glint off the eastern slopes of the Rocky Mountains. Which, when you come to think about it, isn't such a terrible booby-prize.

In the fall of 1939 Rusty MacLean signed up for duty with the Canadian Air Force. That same fall me and my family moved over to Gimp MacLean's to help run the ranch while Rusty was gone.

In the winter of 1940 Gimp got word that Rusty's plane got shot down over the channel, but the coast guard had pulled him out of the water. He wasn't in fighting shape anymore, though, so they shipped him back to Canada. Rusty stayed in a rehabilitation hospital in Calgary for three or four months before they sent him home. It was while we were visiting him in Calgary that Rusty first told us about the legend of the Lost Lemon Mine. Emeline, she smiled at Rusty all through the story, but after we left Em said it sounded like hogwash to her. Cross and Patsy Harmon were sceptical too – but Caleb and me, we swallowed the story hook, line and sinker.

The gist of the legend is that these two Americans, Blackjack and Lemon, along with a couple Stoney Indian guides, broke off from a party of prospectors and stumbled onto a motherlode. This happened in the fall of 1868. Blackjack and Lemon got to squabbling about whether to over-winter near the mine, or ride out to civilization and come back in the spring. While Blackjack was sleeping, Lemon settled the argument by splitting his partner's skull with an axe.

The two Indian guides, they saw what happened. For the rest of the night they hid in the bushes hooting and gibbering like a pair of spooks. That pretty much frazzled Lemon's mind. At first light he saddled his horse and skee-daddled south to the Tobacco Plains in Montana.

After Lemon left, the two Stoneys cleaned up the mess. Then they went and told Chief Bearspaw what had happened and he put an Indian curse on the place.

Although the fancy mining experts claim there's no gold along the eastern slope of the Rockies, Lemon packed a hefty moosehide poke full of nuggets – $27,000 worth – down to Montana with him. That gold was real enough to convince a bunch of fellows to ride north with Lemon the next spring. Ever since he'd murdered his partner Lemon hadn't been quite right in the head, though, and the farther north he travelled, the loonier he got. Neither Lemon, nor anybody else could find that gold mine again – and lots of folks have looked, including some of Chief Bearspaw's kin.

All this was supposed to have happened in the mountains west of the Porcupine Hills, and the people around here have never forgot the legend. We're always keeping a lookout for signs of the Lost Lemon Mine.

A month or two after Rusty got out of the hospital, in June of '40, Cross Harmon got hold of me and Rusty to set up a secret meeting with us. At that time Cross was working for the widow Beckett. Cross said that he and Mrs. Beckett had mapped out a sure-fire plan to make her and us all wealthy. Cross wanted to meet with me and Rusty near the headwaters of Willy Crick where he would show us a map, and where we could discuss his and widow Beckett's scheme. He said we could probably guess what the scheme was, but we'd get into the details out where it was peaceful and quiet.

Well me and Rusty both knew that Jasper Beckett had been a big fan of the Lost Lemon Mine – there was a lot of folks figured that was where Jasper got the cash to buy his place in the first place. Heck, he was out scouting in the mountains the very day his horse fell and crushed him.

No sir, there wasn't much doubt that Cross and Mrs. Beckett had found a map tucked away in Jasper's stuff – a map to Blackjack and Lemon's lost mine. Cross didn't want the word spread around, so he wasn't going to tell us before we were safely out in the boonies.

I don't know why Cross was worried about us spilling the beans. Me, I only told Em and the kids and no more than half a dozen others that we'd soon be swimming in Lemon's yellow gold; and I know for a fact that Rusty didn't tell more than his dad and Fred Wallace about the map; and my dog, Caleb, he's so close-lipped that I'm darned sure he didn't speak the word gold even once to anyone.

Me and Rusty decided to surprise Cross by setting up the Willy Crick camp a day ahead of schedule. After fetching a buggy full of prospecting supplies from Fred Wallace's general store, we piled that and some more gear onto a couple pack-horses, mounted our saddle ponies and rode west. By six o'clock that evening we had a tidy camp built between a heavy timbered hillside to the east, and Misty Mountain to the west. Our tent was pitched in a sheltered spot within a couple rods of Willy Crick.

After enjoying a stomach-stretching feed of steak and beans, Caleb and me and Rusty lounged around our campfire. Caleb gnawed a bone, I enjoyed a plug of chewing tobacco and Rusty puffed on his pipe. A barefaced thief of a whisky-jack was there too. He sat on a pine branch upwind of us and the fire, muttering to himself and waiting a chance to snitch some scraps.

By the time I started my fourth scotch the sun had settled behind Misty Mountain, and the evening sky was dulling to a whisky-jack grey. The air was still summer warm though. I spat into the campfire and commented that this prospecting for gold was one heck of a great life. Rusty exhaled a long sigh of sweet-smelling pipe smoke and said he liked it too. Caleb glanced up from his T-bone. As my dog licked his lips to agree, the whisky-jack swooped down. But Caleb clapped a paw on his bone and the thief had to flit back to his branch empty clawed.

While Caleb resumed gnawing, me and Rusty started discussing what we planned to do with our share of Lemon's gold. Rusty said that he'd use his share of the loot to buy a neat, tidy little ranch. Then he'd buy a hundred head of purebred, horned-Hereford cattle and a dozen Thoroughbred horses. He'd run the cattle on range and run the horses in the chuckwagon races during the summer, and feed everything good green alfalfa-mix hay in the winter.

I chuckled and told Rusty that with the pile of gold we were going to dig up, he could afford a lot more than a hundred head ranch and a few fast horses. I tried to talk him into something more sensible, but Rusty stuck to his guns. He claimed that a wealthy man shouldn't waste his time working and worrying over a great big spread.

I couldn't help but shake my head. Me, I had more ambition than enough when it came to deciding what I'd do with my gold. But before starting my spiel, I took a long sip of Scotch to buck up my vocal cords. I let the liquor simmer over my tobacco before swallowing the mellowed drink. Then I leaned forward, elbows on my knees, and proceeded to tell Caleb and Rusty and the whisky-jack what I had in mind for my share.

I figured I'd start out buying the Rocking P, the a7, the Waldron and 7U Brown's old place and most of the other big ranches in the Porcupine Hills. I'd put together the biggest, sweetest spread in southern Alberta. And I'd run a herd of ten thousand black-baldies – I wouldn't allow any other cattle to run on the place but those Hereford-Angus crosses. I'd put Caleb and Emeline and the kids up in a new house where there was a bedroom and a bathroom for each one of them, maybe even two bedrooms and two bathrooms each. Just to make sure Em was happy, I'd get her something extra special – maybe one of those motorized chainsaws. She'd need one anyway, to cut enough firewood to keep that big house warm.

Well, it must've been past the whisky-jack's bedtime about then, because he ruffled his feathers and drifted silent as an ash-grey ghost into the shadowing timber.

But I wasn't finished my ambitions yet. I told my remaining audience that I figured on having all kinds of hired help: good natured, good looking women to ride over the hills with me; and mechanically minded, even tempered, ugly brutes to run the haying equipment. And when I got too old to tackle anything more strenuous than signing campaign cheques, why then I'd get the Prime Minister to appoint me a western senator.

Rusty shook his head in amazement. He said he never would have guessed that a fellow like me had such glorious ambitions.

I smiled at the compliment, but just then a shifting breeze drifted campfire smoke into my face. My stinging eyes started to water so I excused myself, stood and stepped into the timber for a breath of fresh air.

Leaning my shoulder against a cool, dusty-smooth aspen trunk, I stood quiet and listened to Willy Crick rush and gurgle close by. Our horses were hobbled in a meadow above camp. I could hear their neck-bells tinkling as they grazed. Our flickering campfire daubed an orangy-yellow blush across the tent's front and over Caleb's resting head and ears and shoulders.

Rusty yawned, turned and stooped through the triangle door into the tent. When he fired up our coal oil lantern, the tent lit up like a square-sided, peak-topped light bulb. As Rusty moved around inside the lighted tent his muffled grey shadow darkened each time he brushed against the near side canvas. It reminded me of a chick in a candled egg.

I sucked in a long, deep breath of night air . . . and almost toppled over. A sickening whirlpool started swirling inside my head. It churned all the way down into my guts then twisted around and started back up through my stomach heading for my throat.

After losing most of my supper behind the poplar's trunk, I stumbled back to camp and slumped down in front of the fire.

When my stomach settled, and my eyes stopped doing circuits, I saw that Caleb hadn't even noticed my difficulties. My dog was dozing in front of the fire with his muzzle and paws resting on top of his precious T-bone.

Rusty stooped out of the tent and I couldn't help but stare. The glow from the fire drained the red from all but the edge of his hair, leaving the middle a sickly lemon-yellow. The flickering firelight twisted Rusty's smile. He raised an axe above his head and hacked down – splitting a poplar block with one loud whack. Caleb woke up. He lifted his head, gave us both a glance then settled his chin back onto his paws.

Whew! My whoozy mind had been playing tricks on me. For a second I'd figured I was watching a replay of Blackjack's demise: with Rusty acting as Lemon, and Caleb playing the fellow who ended up with a permanent split personality.

Rusty chopped another block, set the split wood on the fire and sat down next to me. He picked up our bottle and offered to pour me another shot of Scotch. I declined. I'd damned sure had enough.

Rusty pulled out his Buck knife and started shucking long white slivers off a chunk of poplar. When I asked him what he was whittling Rusty shrugged and said, "Nothing . . . an axe handle maybe. Naw. Nothing."

He said that he needed to keep busy – keep his mind off things. Rusty said his bad leg was bothering him and that made him think about the war.

I asked if it'd help to talk about it, but Rusty said, "No. Not yet anyway, but thanks for asking." And he really started stroking his knife across the lumber.

Dozens of white strips had curled and dropped around Rusty's boots when he snarled, "God-damned leg, quit you're god-damned itching!" Rusty reversed his grip, raised the knife and jabbed it down – "Thunk!" – sinking the point deep into his left thigh. Caleb's head jerked off his paws and his startled eyes followed Rusty as he stood up and limped back and forth in front of the fire.

Even though I knew that Rusty's left leg was wood, it was still upsetting to see it sporting a fresh-planted knife, with the blue jeans bunched and wrinkled above the blade. For a couple minutes Rusty stomped around cussing his god-damned ghost leg for having an itch that couldn't be humanly scratched.

After walking his troubles off, Rusty levered the knife out of his leg and sat back down. He set his elbows on his knees, cupped both hands under his chin and proceeded to study the fire. Caleb stopped staring at Rusty, sighed a dog's sigh and pointed his resting nose at the campfire too.

I don't know how long the three of us sat there gazing into the flickering flames, each of us dreaming our separate dreams, but the fire was glowing coals when I finally yawned and stretched and said that maybe we'd best hit the sack.

The fellow beside me, he yawned, too, and agreed that was a good idea. But not with Rusty's voice! And when I looked, I saw that the yellow-mustachioed character wasn't wearing Rusty's face either.

"Who in blazes are you?" I asked.

The fellow canted his head to one side and wrinkled his brow. Then he reset his floppy grey hat and said, "Being as we've been partners for nigh on ten years, you should know who I am without having to ask."

I asked again anyways and he answered, "Lemon," he said. "You know damn well my name's Frank Lemon."

Well, after hearing that name I figured I had to be dreaming, so I checked around the camp. But everything was there – tent, shovels, pans, axes – right where it was supposed to be. I rubbed my eyes and studied the fellow again. Unfortunately he hadn't changed, so I asked him. "If you're Lemon, am I supposed to be Blackjack?"

The fellow sniggered into his yellow moustache. "Hell no," he said. "That there is Blackjack." My eye followed his pointing finger right to my sleeping dog.

Before I had time to ponder that unusual revelation, Lemon leaned toward me and whispered that Blackjack was figuring on running out on us. He said that our partner had gathered enough gold to buy a little ranch for him and his Montana sweetheart – and that was all he wanted out of the deal.

My eyebrows lifted. That didn't seem too smart to me, and I said so.

Lemon nodded his head. He said he felt the same way, but if Blackjack got away with the poke of gold he had clamped between his teeth, in no time there'd be prospectors digging holes all over the Porcupine Hills. I'd be lucky to get out with enough glitter to buy two thousand acres of jack-pine pasture and a hundred Jersey milk cows.

I looked closer at Blackjack and saw that the black-bearded fellow had a long skinny moose-hide poke, bumpy tight with nuggets, clasped in his hand.

Lemon leaned so close that I could smell his rank breath (a prospector doesn't have much time for brushing his teeth I guess). He whispered, "We're gonna have to do something about Blackjack. And soon," he said. "Before morning."

I envisioned an axe dripping with Blackjack's blood, and I protested, "W-we can't do that. We can't kill him."

Lemon rocked back on the log and sniggered. Then he leaned forward again. "I don't want killin' any more'n you do," he said. "Killin' will only be our last resort, if'n you," and here he poked a bony finger in my chest, "if'n you can't steal Blackjack's gold poke away from him."

"M-me!" I said. "Why do I have to steal it?"

Lemon chuckled and asked me if I wanted to wield "the last resort" instead. He hoisted a wicked looking, double-edged axe. Lemon licked his thumb and stroked it across a glistening edge. I saw his point right away.

I eased down onto my hands and knees and started crawling towards the dozing Blackjack. When I was within a couple feet, Blackjack's eyes flicked open. I dived on him and wrapped my arms around his neck. Blackjack whined and squirmed as I tried to jerk the moosehide poke away. I couldn't hold it though, or him, and Blackjack scrambled back between my legs.

The tussle had me sucking in big gusts of air. I turned on hands and knees to face Blackjack; but there stood Caleb, glaring at me and gripping a T-bone in his teeth. I looked over to where "Lemon" had been sitting. There was nobody there.

About that time Rusty popped his head out the tent. "What's all the commotion about?" he asked.

"Well Rusty," I said, "I truly hope that Caleb and me just had ourselves one humdinger of a bad dream."

Caleb looked like he was harboring a different story, but he wasn't about to drop his precious bone to tell it. Rusty, being a bachelor, has never liked getting involved in family squabbles. He shrugged and ducked his head back inside.

After the tent flap dropped shut I heard someone snigger in the bush.

When I turned, I saw a fellow in a floppy hat high-step his way from behind a wild-rose bush and out into the moon-blue timber. He was packing a glittery double-edged axe.

The fellow eased in behind a willow bush and stared toward our dwindling fire; he grinned like a blood-crazed weasel with his star-glittering eyes spinning both ways.

Shivery cold tingles slithered up my backbone. I scrambled over to the woodpile, latched onto our camp axe and split every block of poplar wood we'd gathered. One after another I piled the chunks on the coals, until I'd built a snarling, high-blazing fire that flicked yellow-orange light a hundred yards into the timber. While I kept an eye on the surrounding trees, Caleb backed out of hair-singeing range to a spot where he could keep an eye on me.

Neither of us got any sleep that night, but at least both pairs of bleary eyes survived to watch the morning sun shine on Misty Mountain.

Cross Harmon showed up around lunch time. He was surprised, real surprised, by our camp and supplies and gold mining gear. We were surprised too, when the map Cross spread out on the grass wasn't a yellowing, hand drawn original with a big X to mark the spot. It turned out to be an Alberta lease department range map, with square grids and blue-grey scribbles outlining elevations, cricks, meadows and fences.

Cross and the widow Beckett's sure-fire scheme didn't have anything to do with the Lost Lemon Mine. It involved us three getting together to buy the lady rancher out – lock, stock and barrel. Cross had wanted to meet us at the head of Willy Crick because that was the west end of the Becketts' forestry grazing range. From there we could ride east to the buildings and get a feel for the place we'd be buying.

Caleb and me and Rusty were sure disappointed. We'd intended on buying a ranch with Lemon's gold, not dicker for one with borrowed money. We were so down-in-the-mouth disappointed that it wasn't the right time for Cross to be presenting a proposal to us.

After we turned him down, Cross rode home by himself and ended up making a solo deal with Mrs. Beckett.

Caleb and me and Rusty stayed up in the mountains a couple more days, dipping and swirling our gold pans in likely looking streams. But we didn't find a speck of color.

Almost Forever

Me and the wife have had the store-bought, artificial variety for years now, but when our boys were growing up there was only one kind of Christmas tree: the kind with real bark, and real bubbles of sap that stick to your hands, so your tongue tastes spruce-minty after you chew your fingers apart; the kind of tree that sheds real spruce needles on the rug, sharp-ended needles that poke through your wool socks into your bare feet.

My memories of those old days aren't all painful, though. The outdoorsy smell of a fresh-cut blue spruce still brings to mind one of my all time favorite Christmases.

For over a month Caleb and the boys had been pestering me to get a tree, and Em had been after me for a week, so when Rusty MacLean came over and asked, "Wouldn't it be a good idea to get a tree before the New Years?" well, I didn't get a chance to say yes, no or maybe.

Caleb barked and the boys whooped and Emeline smiled, and all but me and her ran out to the shop with Rusty to find the little Swede saw.

Rusty might've been more interested than usual that year because Em had invited him and his Dad, Gimp, to have turkey supper with us – which only seemed fair since one of Gimp MacLean's gobblers was playing the leading role on our Christmas supper menu. And to give her a little female support around the table, Em had also invited the widow Beckett and her daughter Angela out from Ridgeview.

That winter we were living on the old Slade place and looking after a bunch of Cross Harmon's yearling heifers. The Slade place was about four miles north and west of the Circle X home ranch. There weren't any evergreens to speak of close to the buildings but a draw in behind the house led up to Coal Coulee and a thick stand of north-slope spruce.

Once the boys retrieved their long wooden sleigh from the bottom of our toboggan hill, we headed up the draw towards Coal Coulee.

The boys ran on ahead with Caleb and opened the gate at the head of the draw while me and Rusty tramped along behind pulling the sleigh and talking about cattle prices and about that war over in Korea that some of his old army buddies were fighting in.

The boys were too busy to worry, but Caleb loped back through the snow once in a while to check on us.

Rusty travelled pretty well with his wooden leg but he wasn't near as active as before the war. We watched the boys running and pushing and rolling in the snow, and Rusty said he sure hoped they weren't going to have to fight in any wars, but the way the Commies were swarming over the world he said he thought that wasn't likely.

Me, I was a firm believer that there weren't going to be any more of them ordinary wars after the Korean deal.

"You just watch," I told him. "After this bout in Korea, them Americans and Russians and Red Chinese won't be fighting with guns and cannons anymore. They'll just drop atom bombs on one another and be done with it. And more power to them," I said. "When they're done blowing one another up, us peaceable types can share out what's not full of crater-holes amongst us and our kids."

That's when Rusty told me about this radiation and fallout business, and I wasn't nearly so happy about atom bombs, and I wasn't nearly so happy about the boys' future either.

There'd been a fresh fall of snow overnight. When I watched the boys jump up and topple the white frosting off branches on top of one another, or pat the dry snow into crumbly snowballs, it made me sick to think that someday instead of snowballs they might be tossing lead bullets at other young fellows – it made me even sicker to know that those young fellows would be tossing lead at our boys.

I mentioned this to Rusty and he nodded and we both put our heads down and slogged through the snow without talking.

When I looked ahead again I saw Caleb jump up, latch onto a dead poplar branch with his teeth and pull it down. The boys snapped off the extra twigs and threw the bare stick out for him to fetch. When the stick hit, it sunk out of sight, and that silly mutt bounced through the snow like a muley buck, twisting his head this way and that – then stopped, and sniffed, and poked his nose in the snow everywhere but where the stick landed. Pete had to run over and find it for him. Caleb snapped at the stick but Pete lifted it and threw it again, and the same thing happened – bounce, bounce . . . sniff, sniff, but no stick.

It wasn't but a couple minutes later that Caleb did find some fresh elk tracks, though. They shuffled down off the north slope and for a while the tracks were going up the trail the same way we were. We all hushed up and walked quiet, and farther along we saw half a dozen elk ahead and to our right, on the south-facing slope the other side of Coal Coulee. They were all cows or calves – no antlers on any of them – and they were pawing snow and nibbling bunch grass.

When one of the tail enders spotted us, the lead cow jerked her head up, turned and longstrided away from the trees and up the hill. The others filed in behind her. When the last white-on-tan rump disappeared over the hill, all that was left was a grey line of tracks on the white snow. Those elk sure hadn't hung around to find out if hunting season was still on.

We were into the spruce trees by then, but these were dark, thick, gnarly oldtimers, with only the odd spindly youngster shooting up amongst them trying to reach the light. We kept heading up the trail until we got out of the big stuff and into aspen and smaller spruce.

Right away we found a couple little trees that looked good, but our youngest boy, Dwight, he said, "No way." He wanted us to take the top off of a bigger tree so we didn't kill the whole thing.

Rusty perked up when he heard that. He'd been kind of partial to trees since he'd got his wooden leg. He clapped a hand on Dwight's shoulder and said he was proud of him for making such a thoughtful suggestion.

You could tell Howard and Pete didn't get the idea. Pete especially. Caleb and him kept walking over and staring at this one perfect green cone of a spruce, until finally Pete called and asked me and Rusty to come look at it.

Pete pointed and said, "Don't you think this one would be perfect for the house?" He waved his arm to show all the other trees. "There's lots more trees around here."

Rusty glanced around and said, "Yes there are quite a few but this sure is the best looking one."

Pete nodded his head. "That's right Uncle Rusty, it is," he said. "The prettiest one for sure. It'd look so good all decorated up in the living room."

"That it would," said Rusty. He cupped his chin in his hand. "But how long do you figure it'll be there?"

Pete shook his head, "A couple weeks, but not much longer," he snorted, "seeing as it took so long to get Dad to come on out here."

I thought that was kind of an un-Christmassy comment and I was about to defend myself when Rusty said, "So Pete, how long will this beautiful little tree last, right here . . . if we don't cut it down?"

Pete's eyes opened wider and wider as he thought on that. He glanced back down the trail to where this pretty fellow's grand-daddies poked up eighty and ninety feet.

"Jeez Uncle Rusty," Pete said. "I bet it'd be here for a long, long time, why, I'd say almost forever."

"Well now," said Rusty. "What do you think we should do then. Cut this little beauty down and take it home for two weeks of being fancied up in the house, or leave it out here to live 'almost forever.'"

"We'll leave it," said Pete. He reached out his hand and stroked the tree's thick, even branches.

Rusty said, "Maybe we could cut its top off when it gets a little older."

Pete stared open-mouthed at Rusty. "No!" he said. "Nobody's going to cut my tree."

With his tree-saving sermons, Rusty didn't know what kind of conservating monsters he was creating. When the boys finally did decide on a tree top, it was so high that I had to fight my way through forty feet of snow-coated branches to get to it. And if I broke a branch or a twig with needles on it, they'd yell up at me, "Careful Dad. Don't hurt the tree."

I would've told the little monkies to crawl up there themselves, but I knew that wasn't much of a threat – they probably would've enjoyed the climb.

It was miserable sawing over my head, with the tree top swaying and dropping snow in my face, but I pushed and pulled, pushed and pulled, until the top finally cracked and tipped and tumbled and skidded down the slanting side of the tree – scraping off what snow hadn't already settled on me. Caleb and Rusty and the boys ran over to the fallen tree top. Rusty propped it up like it would sit in the house and the boys "oohed" and "aawed" and walked around it to see which side would fit best into the corner.

They forgot all about me.

I was climbing down, trying to be careful not to break live branches and only step on dead ones. About ten to fifteen feet from the ground, as I was searching out the next hold for my left foot, the branch under my braced boot broke and so did the one

I was holding. I bumped and bounced off a couple branches before I hit the snow.

When he saw me thump down, Caleb ran over and started licking the melting snow-crumbs off my face. The boys, they hated to leave their new tree but they did eventually come over to dust the snow off my coat and help me up. My right ankle had hurt a little when I was lying on the ground, but when I got up and put my foot down it felt like a knife stabbed it. I settled back onto the snow.

Rusty had taken first-aid when he was in the army. He set the tree down, came over and pulled off my boot and socks. First he wiggled my toes and felt around careful and finished off by twisting my foot back and forth until tears came to my eyes.

"Nothing seems to be broke," he said. "It's probably just a sprain."

I must've looked kind of disappointed – it hurt like one of those double compound fractures – so Rusty explained that lots of times a bad sprain hurts worse than a break. I felt better then and told him and the boys that I must have one of "those" kind of sprains.

Rusty and the boys pulled the sleigh over and rolled me on it instead of the tree.

The boys still wanted to find a small tree for Rusty and his dad. It was taking quite a while and they seemed to be having problems finding what they wanted.

Finally Dwight came over. He looked down at me and said, "Since your foot's only sprained Dad, do you think you could climb just one more tree?" He made grabbing hand-over-hand motions. "Maybe if you used both hands to pull yourself up," he suggested. "You could hold the saw between your teeth – like this, like a pirate."

Rusty laughed and said he and his Dad didn't need a tree that bad. The boys said that maybe one of them could climb up and cut one, but both me and Rusty nixed that.

"We've only got one sleigh to drag out the casualties," Rusty said. "And it's already occupied."

For some reason those boys figured Rusty wanted and needed a tree as bad as they'd wanted one themselves. Anyway Dwight asked Rusty would it be good enough if they cut the top off a smaller tree for him – one they could reach from the ground. Rusty said sure but that his Dad and him really didn't need a tree.

That's when Pete stepped up. "Uncle Rusty," he said. "You and Uncle Gimp could have m-my special tree . . . if you just took the very top."

Rusty smiled at Pete and touched his shoulder. "That's really nice Pete. Thank you, but there's no way I would cut your tree . . . " Rusty's brow furrowed and then he grinned. "But," he said. "Why couldn't we make it a decorated Christmas tree anyway – right out here?"

Pete and the rest of us looked kind of puzzled.

"We could bring decorations out here for the tree," Rusty said. "We could make some out of paper or wood or maybe even out of flour and water like those . . . whatever they were . . . that you boys made at school for your Mom's tree last year."

A whisky-jack swooped over and perched on an aspen branch above us. His grey head swivelled back and forth as he checked to see whether we had any food. Howard looked up at the bird. "Why don't we hang stuff on the tree," he said, "that the birds and the squirrels, and maybe even the elk would eat? Kind of like decorations, and presents for the animals, all at the same time."

The next thing I knew Caleb and Rusty and the boys had left me lying on the sleigh and they all ran over to that perfect little tree. They looked it over and I heard them planning the kinds of edible decorations they could make. Howard said they could hang a whole cob of dried corn, but Pete said no, it'd be too heavy for the branches and Dwight said it might work if they sliced a cob crossways into nice round yellow pieces, and Rusty said that maybe a couple carrots dangling down would look good. Caleb, he came up to the tree and sniffed a low branch, and somebody said they should hang scraps of meat and gristle on the tree for the coyotes – and maybe even Caleb could have some.

Then they talked about mixing up flour and salt and water to make paste angels, and this all went on so long that it was getting dark and I was awful cold lying there. I was about to holler over and tell them that we'd best be going when Rusty said it himself, and him and the boys started off towards home to get making the decorations, and Caleb, my own dog, was way out front, and if I hadn't yelled real loud and quick they would have darned sure left me, and the tree I'd risked my life to cut, probably all night, because once she heard about the plan, Emeline would've got all excited and been planning decorations too.

When they came back, Rusty appeared a little sheepish but the boys and Caleb just looked peeved. Rusty heaved the big tree over his shoulder and started limping back. The boys grabbed the sleigh's tow rope and ran off down the trail in such a hell of a hurry that I swear that was about the fastest, scariest trip I ever made – lying on my back, staring through the fast-flicking branches at the dark, star filling sky, the sled hissing over the snow, tipping and turning, with my crippled foot barely skimming past jutting roots and tree trunks.

Every once in a while I'd tell them three boys to slow down and they'd laugh and say they sure hoped the toboggan didn't slide off the trail and over the coulee bank – so I didn't complain for another minute or so. Finally, just past the gate, they ran out of breath trying to pull me and talk about Christmas decorations at the same time, and they slowed to a walk.

That last part of the trip was nice, lying there studying the lay of the stars and looking off to the north where there was just a hint of Northern Lights – streaky, flickering patches of red and blue and green.

I got to listening to the boys talking and decided to throw in my two bits worth. I said they could probably get their mother to bake some of her macaroons, with a string in the top, and with food color in them so they were red or blue or yellow. The boys thought that was a grand idea – they could eat that kind of decoration. When they stopped to argue about which colors Ma should use, Rusty and the tree caught up to us.

Once we got out into the open we could see Em had lamps lit in both the kitchen and the living room. We saw her come to the window and peer out a couple times before she finally saw us. We were through the yard gate by then. Em opened the door and stepped down two steps before calling, "What's the matter? Is one of the boys hurt?" Rusty held his hand up and told her not to worry. When he said I'd just sprained my ankle, Emeline looked mighty relieved. "Bring him on up," she said. "I'll get an ice pack."

Even before Em finished doctoring me, the boys told her what they planned to do, and she got all excited. Em loves Christmas. She even liked my idea of colored macaroons, and she thought up a couple ideas of her own – gingerbread Santas and colored gelatin balls.

By Christmas day my ankle had healed enough that me and Caleb could drive into town to pick up the widow Beckett and Angela. They were the only black family for miles around. Mrs. Beckett had been married to that real gentleman of a rancher, old Jasper Beckett, and she was a lady through and through herself, but she wasn't too proud to come out to a hired hand's Christmas dinner.

Only a couple minutes after we got back, Rusty and Gimp MacLean pulled into the yard too. While Mrs. Beckett and Angela went inside to help Emeline, Rusty and Gimp stayed outside to help me feed. Seeing as it was Christmas day, we forked out double rations to the horses and the heifers.

Emeline had made a nice hot sipping mix with homemade raspberry wine and cloves and cinammon and a dash or two of rum to fortify it. Us males sat around in the living room and visited and sipped while Em and the Becketts were in the kitchen making the supper fixings.

When it came time to take the decorations out to Pete's tree, I was surprised that even old Gimp decided to come. Me and him and Rusty we stumped along at the back; Caleb and the boys led the parade; and, in between us males, Em and Mrs. Beckett and Angela pulled the sleigh. Me and Rusty'd offered to take it, but I don't think Emeline trusted us with her precious load. They had so many decorations piled on, that sleigh was as heavy as when it was packing me.

Everybody'd brought something for the tree. Along with a dozen carrots, Rusty'd whittled and painted three wood soldiers and a doll. They were for the boys and Angela to keep afterwards if they wanted. Mrs. Beckett'd made candied crab apples and popcorn balls. Angela, she strung a fifteen foot rope of cranberries and another one of popcorn. Em's jelly balls hadn't held together so the boys ate them, but she brought her ginger-bread Santas and a whole lot of pretty colored macaroons (I considered them partly my contribution as well as the dozen porkchop bones I brought for Caleb to share with the coyotes). The boys, well, Dwight, had cut up his corn cob, and they'd all made decorations out of dough – I could tell the angels and airplanes – with colored sugar sprinkles on them. Old Gimp brought a little steeple church that he'd made out of shiny horseshoe nails.

There was so much stuff that Pete was worried it would break his little tree. And once we got there, it did look like too much weight, so the heavier stuff got loaded onto another bigger spruce. But we hung the popcorn and cranberry strings and at least one of everything else on Pete's tree – and all the colored macaroons, because they were light. Caleb carried a tight little spruce cone over to me and Gimp set it inside his horseshoe nail church.

Once the tree was decorated, we stood around or walked around and marvelled at how beautiful it was, and then Mrs. Beckett and Angela and Em started singing carols, and lordy they sounded wonderful – that Angela was sure named right because she had an angel's voice – high and clear and strong. Rusty, he joined in and so did his Dad, and pretty soon me and the boys were singing too – even Caleb added an "oww-oww-whoo" that didn't sound too bad.

A couple squirrels chattered along with us, and some jays and magpies, and a little flock of chicadees, they flew over just before the coyotes joined in.

When the sun settled behind the mountains, Emeline said not to worry about the turkey, that it wouldn't be ready until late, so we kept on singing and telling stories until it was dusky dark. We hadn't brought a star for the top of our little tree, but we had millions of them over our heads. The sky was velvet black with the stars shining like sharp bright points, like they get in the cold mountain air. Then the northern lights started up – throbbing reds and blues and greens that shimmered and shone in the north sky and reflected on the snow and on our faces and on the tree.

May the good Lord strike me dead if that wasn't the most beautiful sight I ever did see. The macaroons on the tree glowed as if they had tiny lights inside them, and the cranberry string glittered purply-red and the popcorn strings reflected the bright reds on Rusty's painted soldiers and Mrs. Beckett's candied apples, and the nail points and angles in Gimp's little church glittered and sparked like it was afire. With the Northern Lights flashing stronger above, it seemed like the whole darned world was celebrating with us.

It was too much for Angela. She started singing again. Her voice was so strong and so clear it sounded like it would reach the stars, the rest of us stood quiet around the tree and just listened:

> O Holy Night,
> The stars are brightly shining,
> It was the night of our dear Savior's birth. . . .

Brahma

Have you ever watched those big hump-shouldered Brahma bulls that buck and spin, and smack rodeo cowboys into the arena dust? Did you ever wonder what kind of cows could birth such pug-ugly characters? Well, believe me the female of the species can be just as ornery as the male.

For too many years my boss Cross Harmon's favorite cow was a long-eared, brockle-faced Brahma. Lord knows why Cross got attached to such a miserable critter – maybe just because she looked different from our run-of-the-mill Herefords – but, for whatever reason, Brahma spent her lifetime roaming the Porcupine Hills and tormenting my dog Caleb and me.

Every fall, the first day of roundup, Caleb and me would be out scouting the Circle X range and ten dollars to a doughnut we'd stumble onto that hump-shouldered cow and her calf – if she'd had one that year. It didn't matter where we went. Caleb and me and my horse would saunter around a willow bush, or a poplar tree, and there'd be Brahma's brockle-face leering at us. As soon as she knew we'd seen her, Brahma'd tear off through the trees with her horny head high and her red tail flowing out behind. And we'd be after her. If we dropped too far behind and were contemplating giving up the chase, Brahma'd circle back and run by us again.

For the rest of the morning we'd be stuck chasing that darned cow through patches of knee-banging, face-slapping poplar and willows.

Right around noon Cross and the rest of his crew would have the main bunch gathered, and they'd be trailing the herd east towards the home corrals. About that same time Brahma would've led Caleb and me on a merry chase way over west, almost to the mountains. Once we hit the forest reserve fence Brahma would high tail it back east again, and that'd be the last we'd see of her.

The first couple years Caleb and me kept searching for her. Eventually though, we'd have to give up and ride, empty handed, back to the corrals. And there that hump-shouldered devil would be – strutting her stuff right in the middle of the gathered herd. Caleb and me'd head over to Cross and tell him what happened, but I could darned sure tell he never believed a word I said about his favorite cow.

"Brahma?" he'd sputter. "Hell's fire man, that couldn't have been Brahma you two were chasing. I was right here at the corrals to take the count, and sure as I'm standing here, Brahma was the first cow to step through the gate. Just like she's been every year since she was a two year old heifer."

Now I'm as stubborn as the next fellow, but after a half-dozen years I gave up trying to explain. But Caleb and me never gave up chasing that hump-shouldered devil. We weren't trying to bring her in any more though; all we wanted to do was hold Brahma up so she wasn't the first cow to waltz past Cross into the corral. But that miserable bag had her timing down perfect. We never did manage it.

I think I mentioned before that Brahma didn't always have a calf with her. Every second spring that no-good cow would come up empty. But when I suggested that maybe we should cull her, Cross, he'd stroke his chin and ponder a moment before shaking his head. "Nope," he'd start out, then he'd give whatever excuse he had for that year and finish up with, "let's give her one more chance."

I've got to give Cross credit for his creativity – the excuse was different every year.

The first time, when Brahma was open at three I couldn't much argue with: "That first calf took a lot out of her."

When she was five, though, the excuse: "She brought in a darned good calf last fall," just didn't cut it. With her third year off, she sure should have brought in a good calf!

By the time she missed at seven Brahma had grown a wicked looking set of swept-up, hooky horns and Cross came out with a crazy: "Those antlers of hers'll keep the coyotes honest next spring."

At nine Cross was getting closer to the truth and blurted out: "She's sure a handsome looking devil ain't she!"

At eleven Cross hit the nail on the head when he admitted: "I've kind of grown attached to the old girl," and followed up with the usual, "let's give her one more chance."

When she was open the next spring, though, Brahma had run out of "one more chances," so Cross changed his tune. He said that even Caleb and me had to admit that, "the old girl, after all her fruitful years ranging the Circle X, surely deserved 'a second chance.'"

We darned sure didn't agree, but I didn't say nothing because I knew Cross figured we were still bearing a grudge against his favorite cow. Caleb though, he couldn't control himself. When Cross swung the gate open to turn Brahma out of the cull corral again, my poor dog covered his face with his paws and howled like a spanked pup.

Her thirteenth proved to be Brahma's unlucky year. Again that spring she was standing in the corral amongst the dry cows. The old girl was starting to show her age. She hadn't wintered well – a fellow could've hung his stetson on either of her hip bones. But Brahma's brown eyes still sparkled, and she stood proud with her shiny-smooth horns sweeping high above her grizzled face. She was gazing around the corral like an aging Marie Antoinette at a revolutionary ball when Cross finally agreed that she had to go.

Caleb and me weren't thoughtless enough to cheer but I couldn't help but smile. I stopped, though, when I saw Cross's eyes start to glisten. He turned his face away from us. Said he'd got a darned no-see-um in his eye, and asked if I'd mind backing the three-ton up to the chute.

Well, I bumped that truck against the loading chute perfectly square; I sure didn't want Brahma having any excuse for not walking right up into the truck.

When we walked around to chase the drys over to the loading pen, Cross was leaning against the corral with his forehead set on his arms. I told him that Caleb and me could load the drys ourselves; but Cross, he stepped back from the fence, shook his head slow as he picked up his whip and said he'd help.

I was surprised at how easy Brahma handled. Staying in the middle of the bunch, she trailed right along with the others, through a couple corral gates and into the holding pen – without even a hint of a fight, just like she wanted to go.

Brahma did hesitate a bit at the entrance to the chute alley, though, and waited for the others to move up first. The cow at the head of the line was clumping into the truck when Brahma lifted her horned head and followed the last cow into the narrow alley.

As the old girl stepped down the alley, out of the corner of my eyes I saw that a couple tears had slipped past Cross's flickering lids. They say yawning's supposed to be contagious. I don't doubt it's the same with tears. I can't think of any other reason why I had to wipe a hand across my own eyes.

About then Brahma stopped and stood on a rising angle, half way up the loading chute's ramp. I climbed up on the stock racks to look inside the truck and see what the problem was. I was almost hoping there wasn't room for the old girl to fit in, but there was plenty of empty space.

Cross, he called something up to me. I looked down and saw the middle of his face scrunched together, with tears just a-streaming down either cheek. Cross's voice croaked as he asked if there was room for Brahma to fit in.

I checked the truck again. It sure looked a lot more crowded than it had been before.

I shouted down, "No Cross, there ain't no more room. You'd best ease that old devil back down out of the way so I can get the endgate in."

Brahma didn't need much persuading to back down and out of the alley. I set the endgate in place and chained it tight.

After my dog and me settled into the cab of the three ton, Caleb winked his left eye at me. I clunked the truck in gear and it grumbled through the yard and past Cross as he swung the corral gate open for Brahma.

My boss was still blinking tears but he was smiling. As that high headed old cow trotted past him and out the gate, Cross Harmon was most likely the sad-happiest rancher in all of southern Alberta.

I suppose, after a while, a fellow gets to appreciating his enemies almost as much as his friends. When we rode out to gather that fall, Caleb and me spent the first morning, and half the afternoon riding all over Cross's range looking just for Brahma – but we couldn't find hide nor hair of her. She never led the herd into the corral, either. That fall Brahma never come in at all.

S*quirrel*

The last forty years I've helped Cross Harmon gather Circle X cows and calves off the forest reserve, but after what happened last fall I don't figure on doing it again.

The Porcupine Hills had been blazing yellow and red up until the last week of October. Then a cold wind whooped down from the north-west. Quicker than dance hall girls can drop their fancy duds, those poplars and willows were left with bare naked limbs and trunks.

Seems odd don't it, how we humans and animals dress up for winter while the trees – all except those hoity-toity evergreens – they shuck off their clothes when it gets cold.

Now, I like autumn colors as much as the next fellow, but at roundup time I never was too disappointed to see those leaves gone. It's a whole lot easier to spot a sneaky old cow skulking behind a bare bush than behind a leafy one.

Anyway, last fall's early gathering went pretty well. By the beginning of November we only needed to find a few more pairs to fill Cross's head count. It's always those last few that are the toughest to roust out, though, and after making some awful long rides searching for stragglers, my good old horse, Rocky, had gotten tuckered out.

That left me riding a horse of Cross's named Squirrel – a little brown cayuse who's as ornery as a twisty nail that's been pounded into the wrong spot. Squirrel is one of those sneaky-smart horses that's always flicking one or another ear back, checking to catch a fellow unawares. When you're riding that little outlaw, you don't just jam your boots into the stirrups and sit back loose and easy in the saddle. You have to balance your weight on the balls of your feet and be on your toes every step of the way. Squirrel can duck or dive or swap ends quicker than a cut cat – and for no particular reason either. A fellow can be sitting in the saddle one second and be on the ground the next, with no inkling of what happened in between.

Emeline detests the little devil but I knew he'd stand up to the long jaunt I had in mind. I figured on riding way out west to the Forestry pasture against the mountains.

After packing a big lunch and a thermos of coffee into my saddle-bags, I stepped into the saddle and headed Squirrel down the trail. Caleb took up his travelling position a fair distance behind us. Caleb's not dumb. To keep from getting himself trampled, my dog always allows Squirrel twenty or twenty-five feet of leeway.

Squirrel travelled at a good fast trot, and in a couple hours we were riding up the seismic trail that cuts across the south slope of "three-mile" draw.

We'd just left a patch of heavy timber and Squirrel'd slowed to a prancing walk when his head snapped right and his ears flashed forward. I looked where Squirrel was looking and saw a couple animals in an open spot across the other side of the draw. I was pretty sure they were cattle, not elk, because one of them had a white face. But before I could be certain, Squirrel whipped around and pranced down the trail in the opposite direction – like he figured we'd gone far enough for that day.

Squirrel swapped ends so quick that if he'd caught me in the middle of a blink I might not have noticed. I was sure he'd turned though, because, instead of walking behind, Caleb was out in front, gawking at us.

I had to really haul on the reins to stop Squirrel and then squaw-rein him around. But when we got back to where I could see the animals again Squirrel sped up and pointed his nose sideways away from them, like he didn't want to see those critters at all. I had to haul on the reins again to get him stopped.

By the time I got Squirrel back to where I could see, the white-faced cow had her head up and was staring our way. Because of her cropped-off ears I recognized the cow right away. She was a big old Hereford that Cross had bought, cheap at the auction mart a couple summers before.

It was darned lucky that old Crop-Ears was big – all the fellows who'd owned her needed the writing space. That old crock must have worn a different brand for every one of her ten or twelve years. We'd had to use a small horse iron to fit Cross's Circle X on the only clear patch we could find on her left side – a spot just in front of her flank.

Crop-Ears was a fence-crawler and a loner, so I wasn't surprised to see that she was still out. The fall before she'd avoided the regular round-up too. She stayed out until just after New Years when she and her calf wandered down to the feed ground on their own. In the spring she sneaked back out onto range before she'd even calved again.

Nobody'd seen Crop-Ears's latest calf up until that fall day, and boy was it a queer-looking duck. Cross always uses red-white-faced bulls but, even from six hundred yards, I could tell that calf was no pure-bred Hereford. It was a dun color, with heavy dark shoulders and a peak-ed ass, and it sure wouldn't have won a red ribbon at the fair for having a straight back. From a distance that calf looked like a long-legged, yearling grizzly bear.

My dog obviously hadn't seen anything to beat that calf either. Caleb stared at it with his head tilted to one side.

I didn't think we had much of a chance of bringing those critters in, but I figured we'd best give it a whirl. Once I'd sighted the easiest route across the gully to Crop-Ears and her calf, I gave Squirrel a touch with my spurs.

That ornery character, first he stared over at the cow like she was a dread enemy, then he tried his darnedest to turn back. This time I was ready for his tricks, though. I reined him around, pointed him down the hill and jabbed him hard with my spurs.

As Squirrel reluctantly edged down into the timber I saw that the old cow was heading down hill too. If Crop-Ears and her calf kept heading the way they were, I guessed that we'd meet them somewhere in the middle of the gully. I was starting to think this job might be easier than I'd first figured.

The hill was steep and I tried to make Squirrel zig-zag his way down. But that crazy horse fought and fought me.

Finally, on the steepest part, Squirrel's hind legs slid underneath him and we started ploughing downhill through the leaves. Squirrel's head raised up in front of me so I wrapped my arms around his neck and held on. As the scattering leaves flew up around us I felt like a kid riding a sleigh in powder snow. We tipped this way and that to curve around and under the aspen trees, leaving a swervy, "S" trail behind us for Caleb to run along. Near the bottom Squirrel slowed, then slid to a sitting stop against a red-berried rose bush.

Caleb loped alongside us and sat down. He looked up at me with a loll-tongued grin, as if to ask if he could have his turn now, sliding the horsey down the hill.

Squirrel jumped up and perked his ears towards a patch of red willows on the other side of the draw. Caleb quit grinning and assumed a point position too. I unwrapped my arms from Squirrel's neck and sat back in the saddle.

Leaves and twigs crunched, and the willows shook as Crop-Ears and her wooly calf tumbled out of the brush. They skidded to a halt less than a hundred yards away.

For a couple seconds we all stood quiet, staring at one another. My ears strained, but there wasn't anything to hear; my knees gripped tight to the saddle fenders; my nose honed in on the musty smell of moldering old leaves.

When the cow finally took a step towards us, Squirrel jumped sideways. I ducked to miss a low branch, and Squirrel took advantage of my slack lines by racing down the gully on a game trail.

Squirrel covered a lot of bushy ground before hitting an open spot where I could sit up and haul on my reins. I yelled "Whoa!", skidded my mount to a halt, and swung him around. Caleb skittered to a stop beside us and turned too.

All three of us watched as the cow-calf pair came trotting down the game trail towards us. Old Crop-Ears was in the lead looking uncharacteristically meek and mild.

I just couldn't figure out what was bothering Squirrel. Unless I was mistaken Crop-Ears was ready to surrender – she wasn't on the fight at all. It appeared to me that the old girl had learned a lesson the fall before and wanted to partake of Cross's winter feed earlier that year.

Squirrel was still inordinately shy of her though. His head was lowered and his front feet were splayed out in front like he was bowing down to some bovine goddess. When the cow and calf trotted out into the open, a leaf-denting snort from Squirrel stopped Crop-Ears dead in her tracks. Squirrel stayed put too, trembling under me like a cornered rabbit. We were in a true to life Mexican stand-off – Caleb and me and Squirrel on one side, and the crop-eared cow and her ugly dun calf on the other.

And it was quiet again. Real quiet.

But not for long, because rumbling down from the top of the hill came the loudest, most unwholesome beller I ever did hear; and then one hell of a racket as something big and unhappy came thundering downhill towards us.

The cow and calf swung their heads and looked back, but didn't appear worried. They must've had a pretty good idea what was freight-training its way down the hill.

I took a good look at the calf: big head, humpy shoulders, a sloping pin ass and curly brown hair on the front end. He sure didn't favor his white-faced mama. I had an idea, though, that he might resemble his daddy – the character who was snorting and crashing through the poplars and willows that very minute.

There wasn't a blessed thing I could do to get away, though. The closer and louder the crashing got, the lower Squirrel settled. He was trembling and sweating so bad he was close to melting like a brown puddle of butter amongst the aspen leaves.

After one humongous "SHNORT!" the crashing stopped.

My eyes were pointed down. Hear no evil . . . see no evil is my motto. (I can't for the life of me remember what that other one is.) I didn't care to look ahead so I glanced sideways at Caleb. His eyes were bugged out and his dog's lips were puckered into a perfect "O." Squirrel's eyes were popping too and his quivering chin had settled into the hollow between his forelegs.

The leaves in front of us fluttered back and forth as something big breathed heavy. It sure wasn't Caleb, or me, or Squirrel. None of us had sucked in a breath since the big snort.

I decided I had to look. I peered out of the top of my eyes and slowly raised my head. When I saw what was standing there I gulped – twice.

Planted in the fallen leaves were two dark brown, wool-sided legs as thick as railway ties. They were attached to the biggest darned bull buffalo I ever did see. My head kept going up and up, and from side to side to get him all into the picture. That black-bearded brute towered over the crop-eared cow – it was no wonder she wanted to follow us out of the country.

That buffalo bull reminded me of a crazy trapper, a monstrous character named Harry Powell, who took a shine to Emeline when we first came to the foothills country. It took more than one camera shot to get Harry into a picture too.

The buffalo's eyes looked as big and cold as a pair of outhouse holes in January. He lifted his right leg and a huge hoof pawed a half acre of aspen leaves into the air. They fluttered up and around him like golden snowflakes in a windstorm. The big bull lifted his other hoof and pawed harder. This time he scattered leaves and dirt up into the tree branches.

One pale yellow leaf shot way, way, way up, flipped around and landed on the top branch of a spindly poplar standing between us and the bull. The bull and Caleb and the cow and calf and me, we all watched as that leaf teetered back and forth. It looked like it might hang on, but then it slipped off and wafted gently towards the ground – just like a tiny dropped handkerchief.

As the leaf fluttered down, the bull's nostrils flared out wide as two rubber boot tops. He lowered his head so that his big, shiny, black-tipped horns were pointing right at us.

Squirrel's ears flicked out sideways, first one way and then the other; Caleb's did the same. I couldn't tell whether my ears were wiggling, but I figured my legs had best do something. I decided on the same strategy I'd used with Harry Powell when he caught me at the ballgame with "his" girl (Emeline). As the buffalo's nose and the leaf touched ground I bailed off Squirrel and headed for the nearest big poplar – Harry hadn't climbed after me and I hoped the buffalo wouldn't either.

I didn't have to look back to know that I was being followed – I could hear heavy panting behind me. I took a running leap for the lowest poplar branch, about six feet up, but I overshot my mark and caught the ten foot one instead. As I climbed hand over hand to the top of that tree I felt something big thump the trunk under me. The poplar shuddered but kept standing. I was so intent on climbing that I hit the top and was grabbing air before I knew it.

I settled back down into a crotch in the top branches and slowly lowered my gaze.

Darned if the first thing I saw wasn't that buffalo bull. He was still standing in the same spot, beside the crop-eared cow and her calf. They were all looking up into my tree. If three bovines could smile, those three were smiling, but they weren't chuckling just at me.

The tree wobbled a bit, and since I hadn't moved, I figured I must have company on my perch.

I looked down and saw Caleb's paws glommed around the tree trunk about three feet under me. And if a climbing dog wasn't enough of a surprise, about six feet farther down was Squirrel. He had his forelegs hooked over the first big tree fork and one hind foot resting on the six foot branch I'd bypassed on my way up. Squirrel's other hind leg dangled free, searching for a resting spot. That's what made the tree wobble.

Well, we must have been quite a sight, because that big old bull stood and studied us for at least ten minutes. He didn't make a move to bother us, though. Finally he grunted, swung his shaggy head around and stiff-loped back up the hill. The dun calf was right on his heels.

Old Crop-Ears, she hesitated for one last look at us, shook her head, and headed back up the hillside too.

The three of us tree-sitters waited in the poplar for a half hour longer, until Squirrel started getting restless. He kicked and broke the six foot branch so that both his hind legs were waving free. Caleb – he's terrified of heights – he was hugging the swaying tree so hard I figured there was no way I could pry him loose.

I had to sneak down around them both, snafoo the axe off my saddle on the way past Squirrel, and fell the tree to get them down. When the poplar crashed to the ground, Squirrel, he jumped up and ran off without so much as a "by-your-leave" or a thank you.

On the ride out we'd left the gates open, so there was nothing to stop Squirrel from running all the way back to our place. When Emeline saw him standing out by the barn, she didn't put the little devil in, or come looking for Caleb and me. Squirrel had run off a couple times before and Em had warned me not to ride him again. She figured it would be a good lesson for us all if Squirrel cooled his heels outside the barn while Caleb and me walked home.

It took the rest of the day for my dog and me to make that long walk, with nothing but rose hips to nibble at along the way.

When I got back home and told Ma what happened, she snorted and said my story sounded like a bunch of buffalo bull to her.

Cross had a real belly laugh when I told him. After he quit chuckling, Cross said that he and Squirrel had made that same trip way out west the fall before. They had run into old Crop-Ears too, and when they'd tried to bring her in, the buffalo bull had chased them right out of the country.

Cross hadn't figured anybody would believe him so he didn't say anything about the incident. He said he still wouldn't repeat his story to anybody but me, unless old Crop-Ears happened to trail down to the feed grounds with her beefalo calf. Then he might consider backing me on my story.

But, neither the old cow nor her dun calf ever did show up.

I don't know whether Crop-Ears could have survived a winter in the high country, but I'm darned sure her son and his daddy did. They're the reason why Caleb and me (and most likely Squirrel) aren't helping Cross gather cattle off the reserve this fall.

"Oh Grandpa!" said Patti excitedly. "Did your horse really climb a tree, and Caleb too?" Her eyes were big; she wouldn't take them off me as she reached down to pet my dog.

"I think Grandpa was telling us one of his exaggerating tales," Katie said to her sister.

"Grandpa," the other little redhead said to me, "We tried to lift Caleb into a tree, just a little one, and he was real scared."

"I know, Caleb is scared of heights," I argued, "I had to chop the tree to get him down."

"But Grandpa," added Katie, "none of our horses climb trees."

"Believe you me, Squirrel's so darned quick he. . . . " the screen door slammed shut and I saw Emeline coming down the steps, so I lowered my voice, "Well, he could've climbed a tree," I whispered, "if he'd wanted to."

"Grand-pa," Katie shook her head slowly and waggled her finger at me.

"At least there weren't any bunnies, or Calebs, hurt in this tale-story," said Patti as she patted my dog's head.

Both girls stood up to run toward Emeline. "Come on Caleb," they called, "Grandma's got us some more cookies."

Scaregoose

It's been kind of a pleasant change having those two pint-sized versions of the old lady around these past few days, and I do love them twin girls dearly, but after a while their nattering does tend to get on a fellow's nerves:

"Grandpa, will you take us down to Willy Creek to catch some minnows?"

"Grandpa, it's been almost two hours now. Let's check and see if the chickens have laid more eggs."

"Gra-andpa! The geese are in Grandma's garden again!"

And when they're not on my case, them two little devils are after my poor old dog.

As soon as they get here, them girls jump out of the car, yell, "Come on Caleb!" and run off around the house to find the busted broomhandle they use for a fetching stick.

Caleb does his darnedest. He chases the stick and plays dodge and touch-tag with those two giggly girls, but I know darn well it's too much for him. My dog's getting too old and crotchety to keep up to that pair of bandy-legs.

Why, just yesterday them three chased gophers all morning and then spent the afternoon running and jumping and squawking as they run through the garden sprinklers. By the time they quit, Caleb's ears and tail were drooping and dripping just like them little girls' red hair. That couldn't've done much good for my dog's arthritis, and last night after the girls went up to bed, Caleb flopped down beside the stove and slept so darned sound I didn't think he'd wake up in the morning.

Of course there are advantages to having the girls around . . . like getting two wet smooches in the morning to go along with Caleb's slurp and Ma's dry peck, and listening to the little-girl chatter that me and Emeline never heard from our three boys, or having them sparkling-eyed girls deliver iced tea and a book out to my lawnchair each and every afternoon, and then plunk themselves down to hear a story or two.

Just the same, spending a whole day with those redheaded fireplugs can get tiresome. This morning I figured Caleb and me'd sneak out of the house and drive over to the auction mart to find us some male companionship. I pulled on my best pair of Justins and my good stetson and went looking for my dog.

I found him watching TV, lying on the floor between the twins. Mr. Dressup was just waving goodbye, but Sesame Street was next up, and that's another of Caleb's favorites. My dog wanted to stay and watch the show but I knew he needed a break, so I told the girls Caleb had to go to the bathroom. The silly mutt wouldn't take the hint and come along peacefully. I had to grab his hind legs and drag him out of the room with his paws leaving skid marks on the carpet. Once I got that whining dog out to the pickup I had to put him in the cab so he wouldn't jump out.

Our timing was perfect though. We stepped into the big auction barn just as Harry Rosen started up his chant, calling for bids on the first pen, a couple of old canner bulls. There aren't many cattle going to market in August, so the sale didn't last long, but Cross Harmon and Rusty Maclean were both there.

Me and Cross and Rusty couldn't visit too easy while Harry was yapping out his prices, but after the sale we had a four-coffee lunch and a top notch bull session. Caleb helped clean up me and Rusty's beef dip buns. By the time we left for home he was full and happy again, and appeared to have got over missing Sesame Street and the twins.

We drove back into our yard about three-thirty five. Before I'd even stopped, Caleb jumped out of the back of the truck and ran around behind the house just a-yapping for the twins.

But them redheaded girls were gone. Emeline said we had just missed them. They'd left with their dad fifteen minutes before. He and our daughter-in-law had got homesick and came back from their trip a couple days early. He told Em that since I was usually griping about the twins, he figured I'd be happy to be rid of them; plus he and the wife kind of missed the little beggars themselves.

Em said the girls had given her extra hugs and kisses to pass on to Caleb and me. She also said they'd left us a going away present. "A Scaregoose," Em said.

"What the heck's a Scaregoose?" I asked.

Em pointed out the kitchen window toward the garden, where my lawnchair sat planted in amongst the rows of peas and carrots. Sitting on the chair was a stiff-looking fellow wearing my best western dress shirt and a brand new pair of Wrangler jeans. The pant's legs were slipped over a scuffed-up pair of old riding boots, and tucked into the dummy's gloved hands was my favorite book, *Riders of the Purple Sage*. The whole kit-and-kaboodle was topped off with my battered, silver-belly stetson hat; and holding the hat up was a yellow, spaghetti melon. The way the melon and hat were tilted it looked like I'd fell asleep reading Zane Grey.

"Geez," I said. "From a distance that darned thing looks pretty much like me."

"What do you mean 'pretty much?'" Em chuckled. "Most afternoons that Scaregoose would be a dead-ringer-double for you."

Just then, Caleb came moping around the corner of the garage. He was packing the tooth-marked, yellow broom stick in his mouth. When he noticed the Scaregoose sitting in the garden, Caleb perked up a little, shuffled over and stood in front of the chair and stared up at the dummy's stetson-topped face. Then my dog commenced to whine: his "throw-me-the-stick-please" whine.

Now I knew that Caleb's eyes were getting a tad weak. But I sure wouldn't've believed that my dog would mistake his master, and best friend, for a straw-stuffed shirt with a melon head. That's what he did, though. Caleb whined a couple times, then raised a paw to pat the dummy's wobbly, straw-filled knee. Even then he didn't catch on. That silly hound sucked in a chest-expanding breath, sighed it out and lay down. He set his nose on his paws and shut his eyes.

Emeline, she'd watched this whole performance too. She couldn't help smiling, but then she gave me a reassuring pat on the shoulder and said she'd make me a glass of iced tea.

Em's mix wasn't nearly as syrupy-sweet as what the twins had been concocting, but I drank it anyway. After I'd finished the iced tea I set the empty glass on the table and stepped back over to the window.

Caleb was still sleeping sound, but now he and the dummy had company. A half dozen geese were nibbling their way around the garden.

There's a pair of wild Canada geese that nest down on Willy Crick every spring, and when their goslings are big enough, that pair brings them up to feast on Em's garden.

The wife counts on the geese coming for the odd visit and puts in a few more seeds at planting time for them, so she never gets too upset when they fly up for a snack.

But Caleb and me and the twins, we all love fresh shelled peas, and though we'd be willing to share, those geese don't appear to know the meaning of the word. All the time the twins were with us, those geese only left us a dozen or so pea pods plump enough for shelling.

So there they were again. Those long-necked, masked bandits were waddling up and down the rows, gobbling peas; and right around the Scaregoose and my dog!

I ran out the kitchen door and waved my arms and hollered.

The geese took a quick look at me, honk-squawked, stuck out their necks and then half-ran, half-flapped across the meadow and back down to the crick.

After he heard my goose-scolding voice, Caleb lifted his head and gazed up at the dummy's melon head for a second, then he dropped his muzzle back onto his paws. My dog didn't appear at all surprised to hear that dummy yelling in its sleep.

I cupped my hand around my chin and studied those two garden loungers, and it didn't take long to figure out something that would surprise my dog. I sneaked back into the house, pulled on my stetson and my good boots, and eased outside. I picked another deck chair off the porch and real careful, sneaked over and planted it right next to the dummy's. And then I sat down beside him.

I'd forgot to bring a book, but I didn't figure the other fellow would mind my borrowing his, so I slipped Zane Grey from between his deer-hide fingers.

Before I started to read, something moved in front of me. I looked up and darned if I couldn't see Caleb and me and the dummy all reflected in the big kitchen window. Caleb pretty much looked himself, but I couldn't hardly tell which one was me and which was the Scaregoose.

I was peering close at the two reflections when something moved again. It darned sure wasn't me so I glanced sideways at my partner; but he hadn't budged an inch. I could still hear Caleb sawing logs, so I looked closer and saw Emeline standing inside the kitchen window, right between me and the dummy's reflection. She was looking out at us.

Emeline smiled her laughing smile and waved at me.

I watched in the window as one of the dummies lifted a hand, grinned and waved back.